Praise for Richard B. Wright

A Life with Words

"A remarkable life told remarkably well. Wright, an excellent novelist, proves to be an excellent memoirist as well. *A Life with Words* is a moving, highly original and deeply absorbing story."

—Robert Fulford

Mr. Shakespeare's Bastard

"A writer of insatiable curiosity and intelligence. . . . A total delight to read." —*Toronto Star*

"Wright brings an easy command of social history to bear, on both life within Easton House . . . and on the squalid, crowded, wonderful streets of London." —*The Walrus*

"The glimpses of Shakespeare are irresistible. . . . Wright's characters are splendid. This little novel lives up to Wright's previous successes and gives readers a delightful foray into England in the 17th century." —*The Vancouver Sun*

October

"A gently persuasive novel, solidly grounded in human observation, propelled by character, imbued with wisdom." —*The Montreal Gazette*

"Wonderfully subtle. . . . Inexpressibly precious." —*The Globe and Mail*

"A lovely juxtaposition of youth and age, adolescent heartbreak and elderly pragmatism. It's Richard B. Wright at his best." —*Winnipeg Free Press*

Adultery

"Quintessential Wright, marked by smooth craftsmanship and understated prose."   —*Maclean's*

"Brilliant. . . . A necessary classic."   —*National Post*

"Wright's style is so clear and unadorned that his writing goes down like a glass of cool water."   —*Quill & Quire*

Clara Callan

"By the end of the book, [Clara Callan] seems beyond mere authorial creation—she seems like a living, breathing human being."
—*The Globe and Mail*

"A brilliantly layered portrait of a life that is not at all what it seems. Richard B. Wright is a master storyteller."   —*Ottawa Citizen*

"A profound, graceful story . . . that explodes with drama and passion. A beautiful and subtle book."   —*The Guardian*

"A most gorgeously involving novel . . . with an ending that pops with surprises."   —*The Times* [London]

"Wright has captured beautifully the subtle seasons that permeate daily experience in Canada's far north. . . . A compelling story of perseverance and quiet triumph."   —*The Washington Post*

"Wright creates a compelling narrative and characters who brim with humanity."   —*Winnipeg Free Press*

"Magnificently realized. . . . A terrific novel."
— *The Montreal Gazette*

ALSO BY RICHARD B. WRIGHT

Andrew Tolliver (One John A. Too Many)

The Weekend Man

In the Middle of a Life

Farthing's Fortunes

Final Things

The Teacher's Daughter

Tourists

Sunset Manor

The Age of Longing

Clara Callan

Adultery

October

Mr. Shakespeare's Bastard

A Life with Words: A Memoir

NIGHTFALL

A Novel

RICHARD
B. WRIGHT

Phyllis Bruce Editions
Simon & Schuster Canada
New York London Toronto Sydney New Delhi

**SIMON &
SCHUSTER
CANADA**

Simon & Schuster Canada
A Division of Simon & Schuster, Inc.
166 King Street East, Suite 300
Toronto, Ontario M5A 1J3

The excerpts from *October*, adapted by the author, are taken from the 2007 edition published by HarperCollins Canada.

Phyllis Bruce Editions, published by Simon & Schuster Canada

This Simon & Schuster Canada edition February 2017

SIMON & SCHUSTER CANADA and colophon are registered trademarks of Simon & Schuster, Inc.

For information about special discounts for bulk purchases, please contact Simon & Schuster Special Sales at 1-800-268-3216 or CustomerService@simonandschuster.ca.

Interior design by Lewelin Polanco

Library and Archives Canada Cataloguing in Publication

Wright, Richard B., 1937–, author
Nightfall : a novel / Richard B. Wright.
Previously published: Toronto: Phyllis Bruce Editions, 2016.
ISBN 978-1-4767-8538-7 (paperback)
    I. Title.
PS8595.R6N54 2016b   C813'.54
C2016-902789-9

Manufactured in the United States of America

10 9 8 7 6 5 4 3 2 1

ISBN 978-1-4767-8537-0
ISBN 978-1-4767-8538-7 (paperback)
ISBN 978-1-4767-8539-4 (ebook)

AUTHOR'S NOTE

In this book are passages from a previous novel of mine entitled *October*. These passages provide glimpses of the two elderly characters when they were young and spending a summer in a Gaspé village. I have included them in the hope that they will clarify the relationship between James and Odette at quite different stages in their lives.

For P again, with love and gratitude

The times are nightfall, look, their light grows less

GERARD MANLEY HOPKINS

NIGHTFALL

James

In the months following his daughter's death, James Hillyer's life collapsed into lethargy and meaninglessness. During those anguished nights, his mind circled around Susan's death countless times, and he found a few scraps of sleep only after the whisky had dulled his senses.

He had endured that terrible year with her following the diagnosis of stage four breast cancer in England in October 2004. And by strange coincidence in that same fall, he had also witnessed the death of a boyhood acquaintance, Gabriel Fontaine, whom he had met by accident in London. He and Gabriel had not seen one another for over sixty years, and Gabriel was still in a wheelchair after a lifetime with polio. Over dinner he told Hillyer he had pancreatic cancer and had therefore made arrangements to be helped towards his death by a clinic in

Switzerland. He pleaded with Hillyer to accompany him to Zurich as a long-ago friend, though Hillyer's recollection was that they had not been particularly close during that summer with his uncle Chester in Gaspé, Quebec, where in his own way he had sought the affection of a young girl named Odette Huard. Yet perhaps out of sympathy for another cancer victim, Hillyer went to Switzerland with Gabriel.

But all this dying had left him with a life so bereft of meaning that he sometimes wished for the end himself, as he lay awake at three o'clock in the morning.

He and his uncle Chester didn't like one another much; his uncle was easily irritated by a nephew who seemed deliberately contrary and sullen, while he in turn thought his uncle was a pretentious ass. Chester was a retired teacher at the Groveland School, where James was then in his second year. Or was it his third? It didn't matter. It was all so long ago. Yet thinking about all this, he could still see Odette Huard. She was fifteen and had grown up in the slums of St. Henri in Montreal, as he would learn. She and her mother and seven brothers and sisters were renting the house across the field from where he lived. She would tell him later that summer that her father, who worked in a munitions factory in Montreal, could not find a flat for them and so they had come to this village to live in a house owned by a cousin. That first day in July 1944, he had watched Odette from his little attic room.

• •

From my window, I could also look across a field to an unpainted house, grey from the years and weather. On that first day, even before I had unpacked my valise, I was drawn to the window by the cries of children and a persistent creaking sound, which turned out to be a clothesline pulley in motion. On the little gallery at the front of the house a girl was taking in clothes, drawing the trousers and flannel shirts towards her and stuffing them into a hamper. The wind was blowing the girl's dark hair about her face and flattening the dress against her body. I could see the outline of her breasts. Sheer delicious torment to a boy in an age when the sight of a girl's breasts, even the outline of them, was rare and therefore precious. Behind the house was a shed and a woodpile and an old car without wheels, which over the years had sunk into the grass, rusted and window-less. Several children were running about; a boy was trying to roll an old wheel with a stick, and a girl was pulling a smaller child in a wagon down the lane towards the gate. She was running and the dust from the lane was stirred up and snatched away by the wind. How entirely clear is my recollection of the Huards' yard on that long-ago summer afternoon! I remember how at the gate the girl veered too quickly and the wagon overturned, spilling the child into the grass. He wailed at once and the girl picked him up and, labour-ing with his weight, carried him back towards the house. The others ran down the lane towards her, but the girl at the clothesline ignored the commotion, and after gathering the last sweater, settled the basket on her hip, opened the door, and disappeared into the house.

That was my first view of Odette, though I soon learned her weekly routine. Except for Mondays, she was away most of the time, and I assumed she worked somewhere. At seven o'clock in the morning, she walked down the lane to the gate. Resting my chin on the ledge of the window, I watched her through the screen. After a few minutes, an old Ford truck would stop and I could hear the voices speaking French, the quick, run-together notes of another

*language coming across the field on the early morning air. There
was another girl with the driver and often there was laughter as
Odette climbed into the truck. I used to wonder how people could be
so good-natured so early in the day. In the late afternoon, the truck
returned and Odette got out and waved goodbye and walked up
the lane, the children running to meet her and calling out, "Odette,
Odette, Odette." A black-and-white dog ran down the lane too,
barking with excitement. Like her family, I also looked forward to
Odette's return, and after she went into the house, nothing else was
left in my day except dinner with my uncle and the long summer
evening ahead.*

• •

When he had been there for a few days, his uncle thought he
was spending too much time by himself and arranged for him
to visit a boy who had been stricken with polio. His uncle told
him that the boy was touchy about his disease and he was not
to say anything about his legs. Above all he was not to mention
the word *cripple*. Gabriel, he said, hated that word and would fly
into a rage if it were mentioned in his company. James didn't
want to meet this rich American brat, but he really had no
choice, and that afternoon they drove in his uncle's little Willys
coupe through the mountains to Percé ten miles away, where
Gabriel was staying with his mother at the St. Lawrence Hotel
and Uncle Chester had become her bridge partner. They played
several afternoons a week in the lounge or on the deck with
another American couple. The war was then in its fifth year,
but it all seemed remote in that little village on the edge of the
continent.

He had expected to see a thin, shrunken figure in a wheelchair, but in fact Gabriel Fontaine was tanned and healthy-looking, handsome enough to pass for the younger brother of a movie star whose name he could now no longer recall. Yes, Gabriel had looked like the actor's kid brother with his neat dark hair and eyebrows. Later that afternoon he pushed Gabriel's wheelchair along the main village street to the wharf, where they saw the tourist boats taking passengers around Bonaventure Island to see the birds. From that first day James could see how girls were attracted to the handsome boy in front of him. They didn't cast a glance at James. In the eyes of the smiling girls, he thought he saw what they were thinking as they looked at Gabriel: What a shame! A good-looking guy like that, but crippled.

When they returned to the hotel, James guided the chair into the elevator and they went up to the third floor. Gabriel wanted to show him his hotel room, where they could listen to some of his big band recordings. Tommy Dorsey and Harry James and Benny Goodman. As he pushed Gabriel's chair along the hallway, they passed an open door where two chambermaids were cleaning a room. One girl was bent over making the beds and the other, a plumper girl, was dusting the furniture. Gabriel began to joke with the girls, but they seemed to be used to him as they talked in French to one another. When the one making the bed looked up, he recognized her as the girl from the house across the field.

In the hotel he noticed the cast in Odette's left eye and he liked it. He saw it almost as a beauty mark suggesting something mysterious. Gabriel said things that made the girls laugh. Life in a wheelchair had not kept him from being funny, and James could see how girls liked that in a boy. He would have given anything for the look that Odette gave to Gabriel in the hallway of that hotel. But after the girls left and he and Gabriel were in his room, Gabriel made fun of Odette's eye. He called her something. What was it? James thought it was unkind, especially as Gabriel had also told him that Odette was his summer girlfriend and they had kissed and fooled around in his room. It was all very maddening. What had the bastard called her anyway?

Thinking about that summer of 1944 was like being diverted by an old movie that only he and Odette and Gabriel were in, and during the dark hours in the winter of 2005 it kept him from dwelling on Susan's absence in his life. Then one rainy April night he couldn't stop thinking about Odette Huard. Gabriel was gone, of course, but was Odette still alive? What had her life been like? Had she married? Had children? Travelled the world or stayed in one place? Getting up, he padded barefoot to the window in the front room of his apartment and looked out at the wet night. Now and then he saw a car passing along Avenue Road. For a year now he had been looking for something to do with his life. Anything to distract him; anything that would at least make his days more bearable. If Odette were still alive, she would be what? A year older than him, that would make her seventy-seven. Good Lord! But still he felt this strange excitement at the thought of doing something that no one who knew him would expect. He would try to find her.

At the window on that April night he thought about his life and how unadventurous it had been. For forty years he had been a professor of English literature, teaching the poetry of Tennyson and Hopkins and other long-dead poets to bored students. Now none of it seemed to help him with this emptiness. His son, David, had moved to San Diego with his girlfriend, Nikki, leaving a fourteen-year-old son and a sixteen-year-old daughter with their mother. They lived on a good street in north Toronto, but still David was no longer an active part of their family. As for Hillyer, his daughter-in-law, Brenda, was now his only visitor. He suspected that his glumness had scared away old friends from his university days. And Brenda was a resourceful and realistic woman who after her husband's departure had returned to her former job as an emergency room nurse. She was getting on with her life and she urged Hillyer to do the same, with her pithy way of describing how to cope with misfortune. "Shit happens, James, and you have to shovel it out of the way and get on with things. The kids are trying to do that and so am I and so should you." On her visit that afternoon he had wanted to ask her what was in his life now to get on with. What kind of things should he get on with? But he didn't. She would only have frowned and told him to stop being the academic who can't see life clearly for stepping on it. Brenda was a tonic in his life, and though she was doubtless correct about his persistent ennui, he still thought "shit happens" was a strange and rather hurtful way to describe the death of his daughter.

Brenda, however, always meant well, and her bluff manner only reflected the earthiness of growing up in straitened circumstances in a small northern Ontario town. Now she was coping with her husband's defection, accepting the circumstances and moving on. She had met a young doctor at the hospital and they were seeing one another, though how serious it all was Hillyer didn't know and didn't ask. Brenda, in fact, was rather circumspect about it. But she faithfully saw Hillyer once a week, usually on Sundays, if she wasn't working that weekend, and he looked forward to her visits not minding her bossiness, surmising that he probably deserved it. After all, Brenda watched people facing death every day in that emergency room and so we should all be grateful for life itself, etc., etc. As she told him on one of those Sunday afternoons, "Moping around the apartment all day will get you nowhere, James. Except to that whisky bottle over there," she added pointing to the bottle of Johnny Walker Black on the mantel. "And don't tell me it's none of my business, because it is my business, James. You and I and the kids are family. We have to look out for one another." He told her then how he wished he were able to be a more responsible surrogate father to Brian and Gillian, but he just didn't have the heart for it. Not yet anyway.

"That's not what I mean," she said. "The kids will be okay. Don't worry about the kids. What I'm really talking about is you, James. I don't like seeing my father-in-law, who, by the way I just happen to love, turning into an elderly man with a drinking problem. Drinking alone is a killer, James, and I know it's what you do to find some temporary release from your grief over Susan. But believe me, it can destroy you." She paused, frowning. "Look. I've never told this to anyone else. But I saw my own father, who I didn't get along with and didn't even particularly like, drink himself into a stupor every day for a couple of years after Mom died. He treated her like shit all his life, but there he was drinking himself to an early death. I don't want that to happen to you. What I think you are dying from, James, is loneliness. Somehow you have to let another person into your life. You have to relearn how to share things with another person. You've been a widower for a long time. What is it now, about twenty years since Leah died?"

"Twenty-six," he said. "It will be twenty-six at the end of January."

"Jesus, that *is* a long time. And now you have lost Susan. Is it doing anything for you, just sitting in this place day after day looking for something in that whisky bottle? Why don't you consider going on a cruise? You can afford it. Go high-end. Stay away from the buffet fatties on the Caribbean trips. Go Holland America or Cunard to the Mediterranean for a couple of weeks this spring. You'll meet a lot of nice people. Educated people. Those ships are filled with women who have lost husbands through death or divorce. And they are not all fortune hunters. Many, I am sure, are decent women in their fifties, sixties, seventies, and they are looking for companionship. You would be in demand, James."

But he couldn't picture himself on one of those cruises, hovering on the edge of the ballroom dance floor on Big Band Night watching elderly people try to boogie-woogie. Yes, Brenda meant well, and now that he thought of looking for Odette as a project, he could imagine Brenda's enthusiasm when he told her. "Looking for an old girlfriend? That's a great idea, James. Why not? Go for it."

Odette had not exactly been his girlfriend, but she *was* someone in his life he had never forgotten, and how many people can you say that about after sixty years? Why was that? Was it because of her loyalty to Gabriel, who after all had not treated her well and left her pregnant that summer, a fifteen-year-old girl who would have to tell her parents? Or was it just her intrinsic vividness that had locked her permanently into his memory. It didn't matter now because the whole idea of trying to find her had overtaken him. He saw it now as a project, a puzzle to solve.

Something to look forward to each day. And when he returned to bed that night, he felt settled in his mind for the first time in months. And he slept through until morning.

But where to begin? he asked himself the next day. Yet when he thought further, was it all that complicated? He would start with the Montreal phone book. But what if she had married and was living under her married name in Chicoutimi. Or Lima, Peru, for that matter. If that were the case, he might never find her and have to accept honourable defeat. Look for something else to do. That afternoon in the public library he was not surprised to discover two pages of Huards, hundreds in the Montreal phone book. No point in even starting there. The best strategy was probably an advertisement in the classified section of a newspaper. He had seen them now and then in the *Globe and Mail*. Somebody looking for a son or daughter who had lost contact with a family. *Does anyone know the whereabouts,* etc. *Reward*. It was worth a try. He would explore those barren regions where someone was looking for a daughter lost to drugs and last seen in 1976. Or a son, who had drifted away one winter night twenty years ago. He decided to place the advertisement in both Montreal papers, French and English, and he called a former colleague who taught French literature to ask if she would translate an English version into French. Anne Sinclair was only too glad to help and seemed genuinely pleased to hear from him. He had last seen her at Susan's memorial service six months ago. When he visited her office the next day, he was conscious of being back in the world again, a world where he had spent most of his life. It was nearing final examinations and the campus was alive with the noise of students. It felt good to be out and doing something. He had emailed Anne the English version.

Looking for Odette Huard who lived in Barachois, Gaspé, during
the summer of 1944 when she was fifteen. She grew up in St.
Henri and returned there after the summer with her family. Pls.
phone James Hillyer at 1-416-006-7776.
Email at Memo@sympatico.ca

Within a day Anne emailed him the French version, and that
week he phoned and placed the ads in the Saturday editions of
both the *Gazette* and *Le Devoir*, paying for five Saturdays.

In that first week he felt like a child waiting for some long-
sought-after mail-order package. Nowadays, he supposed,
youngsters would do it all online, but he remembered, as a
skinny twelve-year-old, mailing off the coupon from the back
of a comic book for an exercise program that would transform
him into a young Adonis. He waited for weeks and eventually gave up, until one day to his delighted surprise, the mail-
man took a brown package from his mailbag and handed it to
Hillyer's mother at their home on Crescent Road. What on
earth was this? she wondered. "Nothing," he said, and took
it upstairs to his bedroom. Inside was a small booklet of ex-
ercises that he did faithfully for a few weeks with minimal
improvement. He concluded that the best part of it all had
been waiting for the magical package. Now he felt a similar
anticipation as he checked his email every day. He hardly used
it anymore, but each morning he had a reason for opening his
little Mac.

After a month with no response, he felt a certain satisfaction
in knowing that at least he had tried to track her down. Obviously it hadn't worked, but at least he could safely assign Odette
Huard only to his memory of that summer, a lively, dark-haired

fifteen-year-old beauty with a cast in her eye, a willful girl with a good heart. But probably gone forever.

Then on the Sunday of the fifth week, the first week of May, he opened his email to send a message of congratulations to Gillian, who had been cast in the school play, a triumph since she hadn't thought she had a chance. A momentous event in her young life. And there on the screen was a message from Montreal.

> The Odette Huard you are looking for may be my aunt. Please confirm your identity with a reference from employer, parish priest, etc. And reasons for seeking her. McCann@hotmail.com

Hillyer emailed Anne Sinclair and told her to expect an email from Montreal and would she please verify his credentials. Anne replied,

> Of course, James. Looking for an old flame? How terribly romantic!! Good for you.

Then he replied to McCann@hotmail.com:

> Thanks for getting in touch. Pls. email Anne Sinclair at Sinclair@ UT.ca. She helped with the French translation of the advertisement. If your aunt is the Odette Huard I knew that summer of 1944, I just want to say hello after all these years.

This was all like a game and he could not help feeling excited. The next morning he got a call from Montreal.

The caller had a pleasant voice with a trace of French, though she identified herself as Danielle McCann. She had phoned Professor Sinclair, who had been very helpful. "She thinks highly of you, Professor Hillyer. I have to say I find it quite amusing that after all these years you'd be taking all this trouble and expense to look for a childhood sweetheart. Professor Sinclair did too. She said it surprised her. Didn't sound like you at all."

"Well, I suppose I always come across as a dry soul."

"I have a notion that this sweetheart might be Aunty Odette. She's my mother's sister. The Huards were a large family, I think ten or eleven, but some died in infancy. I think eight survived. Anyway, Aunty Odette is the second oldest in the family. She lives in Quebec City with my aunt Celeste, who's been handicapped since birth. In many ways she's still a child and Aunty Odette has looked after her for years. They just bought this big house in a ritzy part of Quebec City. Only a few months ago, in January, I think. My mother told me the house cost a million dollars, but she always exaggerates. Aunty Odette was very lucky when she won the Quebec lottery last November. Some of the family said it was twenty million, but my aunt told me it was really twelve. But twelve million is a nice surprise late in life."

"Yes, indeed. And your last name is English?"

"Actually it's Irish, Professor Hillyer. Montreal Irish. My great-great-grandfather came from County Cork."

"Well, I'm delighted to learn that your aunt Odette is still with us in the land of the living. I had a crush on her when I was fourteen. I was spending that summer in Gaspé with my uncle. Odette's family lived in the house across the field from us. I used to watch the kids out playing. One of them would have been your mother, I guess. Odette was just a fifteen-year-old girl then, and we became friends but not boyfriend and girlfriend. She already had a boyfriend though, a rich kid from Boston who was in a wheelchair with polio. The two were almost inseparable. I just seemed to tag along."

"Aunty Odette never mentioned anything about that summer. At least to me. But my mother once told me of the old white house in the field where they lived. Odette, she said, had a job in one of the hotels. She lied about her age to get the job. The family was renting the house for the summer because they could not find cheap accommodation in Montreal. It was wartime, I believe. They were very poor, my mother's family."

"Yes."

"Aunty Odette has had a rough life in many ways. She met a man when she was young. Barely out of her teens, I think. To be honest, this man was not up to much but he seemed to be a part of her life. When I was a child I can remember her bringing him to the house. He got involved in a number of things and made her life difficult."

"Did she marry him?"

"No. She never married. She lived with him on and off but had sense enough not to marry him. I'll get in touch and tell her about you, but I think it should be her decision whether she wants to talk to you or not, though I can't imagine why she wouldn't, but she has been a little jumpy since winning all that money. I don't want to air the details of the family, but some of them think Aunty Odette should have shared the wealth. They think she's being selfish and that's made her a little wary of all of us. Anyway, I'll talk to her."

"I'm going to write you a cheque for five hundred dollars, Miss McCann."

"Well, that was the arrangement, wasn't it? I won't say don't bother. I make a good living as a legal secretary but I'm a single woman and I can always use an extra five hundred dollars. But Aunty Odette has had her share of trouble with men. She deserves some peace and quiet now. She looks after Aunt Celeste and I want her to be contented. She's no longer young."

"She would now be seventy-seven. A year older than me."

"I always liked her, but there are family members who don't. Who thought the way she lived was beneath them. They didn't like the company she kept. And then she wins all this money. So some are a little jealous and resentful, I think, and that includes my own mother. But I don't begrudge Aunty Odette her luck."

"Thanks for all this, Miss McCann."

"That's okay, Professor Hillyer. I hope you get together with my aunt."

That day he paced back and forth in the apartment, sipping whisky to calm himself. But then at ten o'clock Danielle phoned back. She had been talking to her aunt earlier in the evening. "At first when I mentioned your name, she couldn't place you."

He was hurt but said only, "That's understandable. It was a long time ago."

"Yes, it was. But when I told her what you said about the boy in the wheelchair with polio, she remembered. She talked about you and the boy, Gabriel. It all came back to her. She told me the crippled boy and his mother were guests at the St. Lawrence Hotel, but you lived in a nearby village in a house right next to theirs. You would go for walks along the beach. She said you were a nice enough boy, but clumsy, awkward, gauche, maladroit."

"Yes, I was all those things."

Miss McCann seemed not to be listening. "My aunt said

she wouldn't mind talking to you. She began to remember you when I mentioned your friend in the wheelchair. 'Ah, the blond boy. Yes,' she said."

He wrote down the phone number in Quebec City and thanked her for her trouble. Told her a cheque would be in the mail the next day. He thought of the first day he had been alone with Odette. She had Mondays off from her work at the hotel and he guessed it was the one day of the week she liked to get away by herself. Away from the other children and chores. She would tell him later how she turned her wages over to her mother. Her father sent money, but they were always short. So she needed a day off and liked the beach and the long sand-bar that separated the sea from a lagoon where herons and gulls nested. He remembered her on the beach beneath the big iron railway bridge.

• •

On that morning I watched Odette walking down the lane wearing a housedress and a cardigan sweater and those awful Mary Jane shoes with ankle socks that girls wore then. Near the gate she stopped to scold one of the younger children who was following her, pointing back to the house until the child obeyed. That too I found alluring, that blend of maternal concern and sexuality. She seemed years older than she looked, but I guessed she was no more than sixteen. The sight of her that summer morning left me turbulent with desire. Following her, I watched with disappointment as she turned in to the general store. On an errand for her mother, then. I had hoped to follow her past the village to a path along the cliff, where I imagined her stopping to gaze out to sea like some girl on the cover of a romance novel, a girl wondering what lay ahead and where was the boy who would rescue her from her life as a chambermaid and surrogate mother, a boy whose heart was also filled with longing and poetry.

Instead I took the path along the cliff by myself and then followed another down to a little cove where I liked to sit on the rocks. I had discovered the cove the day after I arrived in the village, a secluded haven where I thought I was safe from prying eyes. And there beneath the cliff I was free to indulge my dream of undressing Odette Huard. And so I did in a few frantic moments, the seed of Onan spilling once again on the ground. But as I leaned panting against the rock face, I heard something above me, a rustling among the weeds and wildflowers. Unloosed pebbles were falling through the grass. I buttoned myself hastily, but I was mortified because moments later, glancing up, I saw Odette Huard making her way along the path towards me.

Had she seen me, then? Would she be smiling at the thought of telling the other maid at the St. Lawrence Hotel and perhaps even Gabriel Fontaine? I felt like running along the shore as fast as my legs would take me. Running back to my attic room, from which I would not emerge until the end of the summer. Mrs. Moore could leave my meals by the door. But all I did was stand there watching Odette come down the path. She wasn't smiling; she was frowning in concentration, for it was steep and precarious. As she drew nearer, I could see again the cast in one eye, a slight turning to the right. That was what Gabriel must have been thinking about when he called her his cockeyed little chambermaid.

She didn't appear surprised to see me there. "You're staying in the Moores' house, aren't you?" she said.

"Yes."

"I saw you last week at the hotel. You were with the crippled American boy."

"Yes, I was."

She had taken off the cardigan and put one hand on the cliff face. "It's going to be hot today," she said, as she took off her shoes and socks. I could see the swell of her breasts and the hair under her arms as she stood first on one leg and then on the other. Carrying the shoes and socks, she jumped lightly between the rocks to the little sandy beach, where for a few moments she stood in the water. Then she came back and sat down on the sand.

Looking back at me, she called, "He's very funny, that friend of yours."

"He's not a friend of mine," I said, walking towards her.

She must have caught something in my voice, for she smiled. "Why don't you sit down and have a conversation with me? We're neighbours, aren't we?"

"I suppose we are, yes."

It is not easy for a girl to sit on the sand in a dress with a boy beside her. Either she draws her knees towards her and hugs them with both arms for modesty's sake, or else she stretches them out. Odette stretched out her legs, leaning back on her elbows and staring at the water. I couldn't take my eyes off the sand that clung to her feet. She was looking at me.

"Do you like it here in the village? It can't be much fun. You don't speak French, do you?"

"No," I said.

She shrugged. "It doesn't matter. It's mostly English around here. I'm from Montreal. We're just staying here while my father makes some money for us." She was still looking at me. "What's your name?"

"James," I said.

"Mine is Odette."

"Yes, I know."

"Why is your face so red? It's like a big tomato. Your ears are red too." I looked away. "Maybe you don't talk much to girls," she said. "Is that it?"

"Something like that maybe."

"Well, don't worry, I won't bite."

"I'm not worried."

It was a still morning and a haze lay across the water. Gulls wheeled and squawked. Now and then, over the wash of the sea, we could hear a car passing on the road above the cliffs.

"Do you like it here?" Odette asked.

"Yes," I lied. "It's very beautiful."

"I thought you might say that," she said. "Everybody who comes here says that. And it's true, I guess. But do you really like it here? You don't do anything but stay in that house and look out at me."

Shocked? Yes, of course, though flustered would be more like it. All along then, she had known I was watching her, my hapless moon-like face at the window.

"Yes," Odette said, "I've seen you looking out at me through your little window." Then she did a wonderful thing. A miraculous thing to me. She sat up as if we were already old friends and gave me a quick hug. "Oh, don't take it all so seriously," she whispered. "I'm just teasing you. I don't care really. It's nice to be looked at." Her warm breath in my ear. I had never been that close to a girl. Again she leaned back on her elbows. "I knew your name before today. Gabriel told me."

"Did you tell him that all I do is look out the window at you?"

She laughed. "No. Why would I do that?" I shrugged and

she said, "He wonders why you haven't come back to see him. He mentioned it one day. He likes you. He doesn't get much company."

I was imagining the both of them talking about me.

"That Gabriel," she said, "he's always making fun of Pauline and me, but he doesn't really mean it. It's just his way. He's very generous. He gives us things."

"Like what?" I asked.

She was sitting up now, hugging her knees, looking out at the water. "Cigarettes. Coca-Cola. He gave me a book last week. I said I liked reading, so he gave me this book." She laughed. "It's got some dirty parts in it. He underlined them." I was looking at the turning in her hazel eye. I liked it. "Gabriel's funny," she said. "He plays his dance music when Pauline and me are cleaning his room. He sits there conducting the band, and I always find that . . ." She stopped. "There's a word in English meaning 'very funny.' It starts with the letter aitch."

"Aitch?"

"Yes. Aitch like in hill or hat."

"Hilarious?"

"Yes. Hilarious, that's it." She said it slowly, pronouncing all four syllables. "It's hilarious when he does that." I didn't say anything, and then she said, "But he's brave too. Gabriel will never dance to that music, and that's very sad when you think about it."

"I guess so," I said. "I don't know him very well. I just met him that once. That Saturday you saw us together. My uncle wanted me to meet him. It was all his idea."

She was looking sideways at me, resting her head on her knees. "You don't like Gabriel?"

"He's all right."

Odette then took her sweater and made a little pillow behind her. She lay down and, using a hand to shield her eyes from the sun, looked up at me. It was funny but it all seemed so natural to be there with her. We'd really only known each other for ten minutes, but she had that way about her, a forthright nature that allowed her to enter your life almost immediately. With only a handful of scattered facts to go on, she led the way so that in no time at all you felt free to comment or argue with her.

"Your uncle writes books, doesn't he?" she asked.

"Yes," I said. "Books for children. They're not very good. Silly, really."

She was staring up at the sky with the little roof of her hand across her eyes.

"Well," she said, "it's something to write books. Any kind of books. I would like to write a book someday. You should be proud of your uncle."

Proud of Uncle Chester? The thought had never crossed my mind.

I may have shrugged again or she saw something in my face, for she said, "Why are you such a sorehead anyway? You don't like Gabriel. You think your uncle writes silly books. And all you do in this beautiful place is stay up in that room and peek at me when I'm hanging out the family bloomers." Sitting up again, she gave me a little push, which caught me off balance. I very nearly toppled. "I think you are just not used to girls," she said. "How old are you anyway?"

"Sixteen," I said.

"Ha. I'll bet not. You don't sound like sixteen to me." She lay down again. "More like fifteen, I'd say. Maybe even fourteen . . ."

"Gabriel told you how old I am."

She smiled. "Maybe."

"So why ask if you already know? Just to make fun of me?"

"Maybe."

"Anyway, how does sixteen sound? Like Gabriel, I suppose."

Odette had closed her eyes and now I could look at her as she lay there. "Gabriel," she murmured, "sometimes sounds more like twenty-one." She lay as though sleeping with an arm across her forehead, and this lifted a breast inside that flimsy housedress. She spoke as if in sleep. "Gabriel told me you were only fourteen. So you see I have already caught you out in a lie. The first time we talk and you lie to me." Then abruptly she sat up. She knew that I had been staring down at her. I was angry.

• •

In bed that Monday night, Hillyer wondered what he would say to Odette the next day, and he went to sleep thinking of the sky and the sea and the sand and Odette's pale calves in the water. In case she was a late riser, he waited until nearly noon and then called the number. When he heard a voice say, *"Allo,"* he offered his badly pronounced French. *"Je veux parler avec Odette, s'il vous plaît?"* There was silence and then the voice yelled *"Pour toi, Odette,"* and a moment later the voice whispered, *"Anglais."* Then he heard, *"Oui? Yes?"*

The voice was not exactly unfriendly but brisk, a voice wary perhaps of spam calls and other nuisances. "Odette," he said, "this is James Hillyer. I'm calling from Toronto. Your niece, Danielle, said she was talking to you about me and she said you agreed to let her give me your number."

"Oh, yes. Danielle called me about you. She said you advertised about finding me in the *Gazette* and *Le Devoir*. I couldn't believe it. All that trouble and expense after how many years?"

"Sixty-two."

"My God. Yes, it must be." For a moment there was silence and then she said, "Yes, I told Danielle to give you my number. I said I didn't think you would be after my money." She laughed and so did he. Hints of the old Odette. Temperaments never change. We are what we were, only in old bodies, he thought.

"No, I don't want your money, Odette. It's just good to hear your voice."

"Nice of you to say that, James. I remember you now. I have been thinking of you and Gabriel and that summer in Gaspé. Poor Gabriel. Is he still alive, do you know? Do you keep in touch?"

"No. We didn't keep in touch, but then—I know this is hard to believe—I met him by accident in London, England. Two years ago."

"England, eh? Does he live there now?"

"No, no, Gabriel died that year."

"Ah, I see."

"And how are you, Odette? How has life treated you over the years?

"I'm all right, James. I can't complain. I've had rough times but also some good fortune. I'm sure Danielle has told you about our lottery win, Celeste's and mine."

"Yes. Congratulations."

"Well, you know, it's just luck. Blind luck. But for sure I needed some then. And how about you?"

"I'm okay. Retired now, of course. I was a professor of English literature for forty years. I've been retired for five years."

"That's good, James. I'm not surprised that you were in teaching. I remember how you liked reading as a boy. You were the only boy or man I ever knew who read poetry. I remember you had a book of poems down in Gaspé that summer and you loaned the book to me. I said I wanted to read some of it but I didn't get very far."

"Yes, a book of Tennyson's poetry. Well, he was a bit old-fashioned by then, and many of his poems are not easy to read."

"You know, I don't think I ever gave that book back to you."

"No, you didn't, but that's all right."

"Well, I'm sorry. People should give things back if they're loaned to them. I don't think I understood much in that book, but it was nice of you to loan it to me all the same. You were a good friend to me, James. A little awkward and unsure of your-self but nice to me even though we had little quarrels, as most friends do."

"Yes."

"You gave me some money before you went home that summer. I needed money."

"Yes. I was glad to help, Odette."

Neither spoke for a few moments. She was pregnant at the end of that summer, and he wanted to help her. Fifteen years old and pregnant. And Gabriel did nothing when he told him. Odette wouldn't say anything to Gabriel, but he had. And Ga-briel did nothing about it. Nothing to help her, the bastard.

He didn't expect to tell her. But maybe it was there all the time behind his memories of her. "I'm planning a little trip. A little holiday for myself," he said. "I'm a widower and have been for many years. And then two years ago I lost my daughter to cancer. She was only forty-six. I have a son but he's settled in California with another woman, and anyway we've never been close. So, I'm planning this little trip and I thought of going east towards the Maritimes and possibly on my way stop over in Quebec City. I have only been there once and that was when I was six or seven. I went with my parents. So I was wondering if we might have dinner together one night. My treat, of course. I'd love to see you again."

"Well, I suppose so, yes. Why not? If you're coming this way. What year was that anyway? That year in Gaspé?"

"Nineteen forty-four."

"Yes, the war was on. My father was working in a munitions factory. He couldn't find a house he could afford in St. Henri for ten people. That's why we went to Gaspé that summer. When do you think you'll be taking your holiday?"

"I thought next Monday I would leave. And maybe we could have dinner on Tuesday."

"For sure. Why not? I don't know if Danielle told you, but I live with my sister, Celeste, who sometimes gets a little confused about things. Her mind has never been strong."

"I'll give you a call next Saturday to confirm all this. I think I'll come by train. See the countryside in this early summer weather. I'll give you my phone number in case something comes up and you can't make it."

"Okay. Good. I've got a pen and pencil here by the phone."

"If you give me your address, I could come by taxi from the hotel and we could go out to dinner on Tuesday."

"Okay then. We live at 8085 Avenue Wilfrid Laurier. A big brick house with a white verandah. We only moved in last January. Where will you stay?"

"I've booked a room at the Chateau Frontenac."

She laughed. "Good for you. I'm told the Frontenac is very nice, but it's not cheap."

"It doesn't matter. This will be an occasion for me. I need a change of scenery. Something to freshen up my life."

"Ah. Your life now is—what do you say in English, stale? A little stale."

"Yes, stale is a good way to describe it."

"In French we would say perhaps *banal*."

"That works for me too."

"Neither of us will look anything like what we can remember, eh? Do you still have all your hair, James? I remember a boy with all this blond hair piled up. Or falling onto his face."

"Yes, but it's now white, as you might expect."

"Yes. Good. What does it matter? We're both still here. Poor Gabriel. And he died in England? I hope he didn't suffer at the end."

"I'll tell you about it when we see one another."

"Good. Very good."

"I'll phone from the hotel when I arrive."

"Okay then. *À la prochaine*. That means 'see you!'"

"Thanks, Odette. *À la prochaine*."

When he phoned his daughter-in-law about his trip to see an old friend in Quebec City, Brenda was delighted. "Good for you, James. Male or female?"

"Female," he said. "I saw her last when I was only fourteen."

"An old girlfriend. How romantic." He didn't bother to correct her. What was the point? Everyone seemed to have the notion that he had some old girlfriend tucked away.

"Well, it will be interesting," he said. "To see what she has done with her life."

"Yes. And it will get you out of that damn apartment for a while. This is great news, James. I'm happy for you. The kids will be too when I tell them."

For the rest of that week he kept busy preparing for his holiday: tidying up the apartment, packing his clothes and paperbacks for the train; he went to the bank for money and told them to expect charges on his credit card from Quebec; he bought his ticket and by the weekend he had trained himself to take more care with shaving. Like many elderly men who live alone, he had grown lazy about personal care. He kept himself clean enough, but often he shaved only two or three times a week, now and then cutting himself under the chin in his haste to get past the tedium of it all. Isolation will do that to you, he thought as he carefully stroked his under chin with the blade. By Saturday afternoon his clothes were laid out on the bed and he had put his suitcase out on the little balcony for airing.

That night around ten o'clock he was watching television when the phone rang. The sound of a ringing telephone at that hour was unusual and mildly alarming; he feared bad news; perhaps one of his grandchildren had been in an accident. But when he picked up the receiver, he heard Odette's voice. "Allo. Is that you, James? Have I got the right number?" She sounded agitated.

"Yes, Odette, it's me."

"I'm very sorry, but something has come up. I don't think it will be a good idea for us to be together next week."

"I've got my train tickets and hotel reservation booked, Odette." He was aware that he sounded too quickly aggrieved. But he had always hated changing plans. The bother of it all. And now at his age he hated the idea even more.

"James, I'm very sorry but I can't see you. It would be just too complicated. Difficult."

"Forgive me for asking, but are you all right?"

"I'll be all right, but the next few days is not a good time for you to be here."

What was the point of pushing it? She was obviously in some kind of distress and she didn't want to draw him into it. He remembered Danielle saying that her aunt had sometimes led a rough life. Or perhaps it had something to do with her family and the lottery win. He had read somewhere that winning large sums of money could often attract interference and troublesome behaviour from family members.

"Please don't be angry with me, James. Things in my life are now a little difficult."

"I'll change my plans, but I would love to see you when it's convenient."

"If you could visit in, say, two weeks, I'm sure things will have settled down here. And it will be early June then. A nice time to visit Quebec. You'll like it. Is that okay with you? "

He was looking at the wall calendar in the kitchen.

"I'll call you from the hotel when I arrive on, say, June sixth. And we'll meet for dinner on the seventh. That's a Tuesday."

"Good. And you don't have to pick me up here. I'll come to the Frontenac. I'll meet you in the dining room at seven o'clock."

After he hung up, he poured some Johnny Walker into a glass and got into bed. Something was certainly going on in her life. He waited for the whisky to calm him. Two weeks was not so very long to wait, and on Monday he would make new travel arrangements. Then he would have to do something in the two weeks that lay ahead.

Staying in the apartment now made him anxious. And so he played the good grandfather and on Saturday took Brian to a movie. He and his grandson had been remarkably close for the first dozen years of Brian's life. He had been a funny little boy, constantly amused by the adult world and eager to play checkers or be read to by his grandfather. Hillyer thought he could see a good deal of his younger self in Brian. But over the last couple of years, the boy had become more distant, more closed in. He had never really been close to his father, but now he seemed to be distancing himself from everybody; Brenda seemed at a loss as to how to reach him. And so at her request Hillyer had taken the boy to a Saturday afternoon movie where they watched a young woman, who was really a vampire, lure the handsome young man to her apartment. At age twelve, Brian would have laughed at the clunky plot and bad acting, but now two years later he just seemed restlessly irritated by it all. There was a little sex in the movie, just enough to entice the young teenage crowd without alerting the censors. It didn't matter. Both grandfather and grandson were bored, and they left early for a visit to Tim Hortons.

At the end of the day Brian thanked him politely. Hillyer could see that the boy, while trying to be happy, was finding it very difficult. Still his good manners never deserted him. Brenda said he was terribly sarcastic around the house, but at least with Hillyer he was polite. He was just the age Hillyer had been in 1944 when he had met Gabriel and Odette. Brian's sixteen-year-old sister, Gillian, missed her father more. She had visited him the year before in California but phoned after only a week to say she wanted to come home. She couldn't stand Nikki Martin, the young woman her father was living with. This summer was supposed to be Brian's turn to visit, but as yet he hadn't revealed any great enthusiasm for the trip.

In the second week, Hillyer visited an old friend and former colleague, John Matheson, who was almost the same age as Hillyer. He had been a specialist in Coleridge, but he was now in a nursing home with an oddly twisted face, recovering from a stroke that unhappily had also left him speechless, deprived of words: a cruel fate for a man who had devoted his life to language. He had made his living with words, but now it seemed he could only scribble them on pieces of paper. There were pages strewn on the floor by his bed, the letters half an inch high. BED PAN PLEASE. Another with HELLO JAMES. That afternoon Hillyer sat by his friend's side as he held up a piece of paper that said TALK TO ME. I AM LISTENING. But after an hour John had reached for another sheet of paper, TIRED THANK YOU FOR COMING. Then he had turned his face to the wall, and Hillyer left. John had always been such a polite man. Now he was reduced to grimaces and gestures and bits of paper with scribbled words upon them.

When a few days later Hillyer boarded the train for Montreal, he was grateful to be leaving Toronto. The stroke that had felled John Matheson, however, bothered him, and as the train moved eastward he sat by the window in business class with a cup of coffee thinking of his friend in the nursing home. Anything in life can happen, particularly in the late years. There is never a shortage of personal catastrophes. For the elderly, disfigurement, decline, and death. It was all out there waiting and he knew it. Hillyer in some way was still fortunate. Was this schadenfreude? Maybe. Like his grandson, Brian, he had always been fascinated by misfortune. When Brian was nine or ten, he liked to read accounts of people with terrible diseases. They seemed to fascinate the child. Was it the same with him? Had his visit to the nursing home actually made him happier, more grateful for his own health? He wasn't sure. He only knew that looking out the window at the green fields and trees and the early summer sunlight, he felt somehow grateful. He could still do this. He could still get on a train and visit a woman who had once been a lively and vivid presence in his life. It was, he thought, a small miracle that she had even remembered him. He thought back to how angry he'd been on the beach the first time they had actually talked.

• •

"You're French," I said. "Where did you learn to speak English?"

"In Montreal," she said. "I grew up in Montreal. I'm only here for a while. My father lives in Montreal. He works in a factory where they make gun shells and bombs. He earns good money after being out of work for a long time. This is only our first year here. My father moved us here last October because it's cheap. A cousin of ours owns the house. He works at the same place as my father, but he doesn't have as many kids, so he moved his family up there. I have seven brothers and sisters. Try to find a house in Montreal to rent for ten people. My father is saving money for us, though." She was shaking the sand out of her sweater. "He's coming for a visit next month. I can't wait. He'll bring me some books. Maybe a new dress or a skirt. My father can actually buy clothes for a woman. He buys all my mother's clothes. Not many men can do that."

I felt chastened by her story. Wanted to compliment her. "Your English is really good."

She looked at me as if I'd insulted her, and of course I had. I'd patronized her with my remark, though I hadn't meant to. "I speak good English," she said, "because my father taught me. I also speak good French, but my father says that you need English to get ahead. The English run things in Quebec. They run the banks and the railways and the big stores, Eaton's, Simpson's, Morgan's. You have a better chance if you speak English . . ." She stopped and then said, "My father is an interesting man. I am very proud of him. He speaks English, French, and Latin. He learned his Latin in a seminary. Are you a Catholic?"

I shook my head.

"I didn't think so," she said. "Most English people aren't Catholic. That's why they own everything, my father says. He has no love for the Church anymore. I'm the only one he talks to about it, and it makes my mother mad because she's very devout. You can see that for yourself when she takes my brothers and sisters off to Mass every Sunday. I work on Sundays, but I still go to Mass when I can, but I'm more like my father than my mother. My father was going to be a priest, but he quit. He told me it didn't work for him. He didn't like what he was being told. He liked to read books too and there were a lot of books that he was not allowed to read, and he didn't think that was right. Books on religion and science and philosophy. My father is interested in all that stuff, and they wouldn't let him read about it, so he quit. And his mother and father, his brothers and sisters, none of them will speak to him now. The whole family is against him." She was leaning forward, hugging her knees again, rocking a little. "It will be good to see him and have a talk. It opens up my brain when I talk to him."

It was hot by then on the sand. We looked out to sea and watched the clouds moving in from the southwest. Farther down the beach we could see children playing under the railway bridge where the water was warmer. The big iron bridge above the children crossed a river to the sand bar that formed a natural barrier between the sea and the lagoon, a large tidal pond where seabirds rested and fed on little islands of marsh grass. On the seaward side of the bar was a long crescent of beach that stretched around the bay almost to the village of Percé.

Odette stopped gazing at the children and looked at me. "You should go and see Gabriel," she said. "He needs a friend for the summer and so do you. The boy is in a wheelchair. It wouldn't be any skin off your face to take him out and have a look at the girls and the tourists, would it? That mother of his is too busy with her friends, playing their card game. What do you call it? Bridges?"

"Bridge," I said. "Singular, and the expression in English is 'skin off your nose.'"

"Oh, yah?" she said. "Well then, it would not be any skin off your big nose to be a friend to that boy. And you need a friend too, Mister Sorehead. You can't stay inside Madame La Plotte's house all summer."

"Please don't call me that," I said.

"What?"

"Mister Sorehead."

"You don't have much humour in you."

"I don't like to be made fun of, no."

"I'm only teasing you. Don't take it so tough."

"Hard," I said. "Don't take it so hard."

"Okay. Don't take it so hard."

I shrugged again. She was right. I took myself too seriously, and if I wanted to be this close to her, I would have to learn to parry her mocking remarks and adjust to her offhand manner. I didn't know how to talk to a girl, but I vowed I would learn. I knew sitting next to her on the beach that day that I would never be her boyfriend. I was too young, too callow for her; I had already been relegated to the *role of harmless eunuch, the platonic friend, the younger kid who just hangs around sniffing. But it was better than nothing. Being close to her like that, I could still enjoy her slightly rank smell, the sight of a mole on her not quite clean neck, and that cast in her hazel-coloured eye, the sand between her toes.*

As we started back along the shore, she was carrying her shoes and socks and sweater. Walking slightly behind her, I could admire how her feet in the sand lent a shapeliness to her pale calves. I asked her why she called Mrs. Moore Madame Something-or-other.

"Madame La Plotte," she said. "The old bag doesn't like us. She thinks we're just a bunch of ignorant French Canadians with too many kids under one roof. We're always running around the house yelling at one another. She thinks she's better than us, but I'll bet she hasn't read as many books as my father, goddamn her eyes."

"But what does the word mean?" I asked.

Laughing, she turned around and began to walk backwards. "What does it mean? I don't think you're old enough to know that."

I sprang forward and pushed her, the schoolyard impulse of a fourteen-year-old boy who feels challenged or insulted, even in jest, and I regretted it the moment I touched her. She stumbled backwards and fell. "I'm sorry," I said reaching down for her. "I didn't mean it." But as she was getting up, she knocked my hand away.

"What a bully you are for your age, already beating up girls."

I must have looked contrite enough, because she laughed. "Forget it. If I really felt like doing something, I would kick you in the balls. Just see if I wouldn't."

"You can kick me," I said, "but not there, please." We both laughed at that and I felt a rush of exhilaration, for I knew we were going to be friends. I had picked up her shoes and was knocking the sand out of them.

"Tell your uncle," Odette said, *"that you want to go to Percé with him this afternoon. Tell him that you want to see Gabriel again. That you want to be his friend."*

"He already has a friend," I said. *"He has you."*

"Me?" she said. *"A friend?"*

"Sure, he told me you were pretty good friends."

"He did, eh? Well, that's his opinion. We kid around when I'm cleaning his room. But don't forget that I'm cleaning his room. That's not what friends do. That's what people like me do. People like me are just servants to Gabriel and his mother. And to you and your uncle if you were staying at the St. Lawrence Hotel. You're all rich."

I wanted to say that I wasn't rich, that the rich were in another camp where I didn't belong or want to be. But I had come to Gaspé from Ontario by train in a sleeping compartment reserved for me by my father. My uncle wrote books and played tennis and bridge and drove a car. I went to a fancy school like Gabriel's. I badly wanted to be on her side, but how could I? That morning I had to settle for the notion that at least I had established a beachhead, a word I learned from reading the newspapers in the Groveland library after D-Day.

• •

He hadn't travelled by train in years, and as he saw the sign for another small Ontario town, he thought of those Sunday train rides to Groveland School after a holiday. The onset of nerves as the train stopped and he and other boys were met at the station by the driver and a teacher who stepped down from the school bus. Ahead lay another two months of dormitory life with its smart alecs and bullies, and the endless farting. The long talks into the night, the murmur of voices. The prefect's flashlight in their faces. "Get to sleep, you guys." A kind of desolate sadness taking over as he stood in line to board the bus, already missing his mother.

Now so many years later he sensed that he had reached some kind of turning point. Or was it just the green fields and the trees under the early summer sky or the thought of again meeting Odette Huard? Nothing in his life had changed in the last two weeks. Susan was still gone forever. But perhaps those grief counselors he read about were correct. In time deep wounds heal and people pick up parts of their lives and try to put them together again. He knew that Susan and her absence would always be there, embedded in his memory. How could she not be? But perhaps he could learn to live with his loss. When the pretty attendant came by, he ordered a Bloody Mary, and the salmon for lunch with a glass of white wine. Or maybe two? She smiled at him. "We'll look after you, sir."

Odette

From the kitchen she could hear the squawking Daffy Duck and that loud-mouthed carrot-crunching rabbit. "What's up, Doc?" She put the last of the breakfast cups and plates in the dishwasher and, walking to the hallway at the bottom of the stairs, called up to her sister to turn down the television or close the door. A moment later Celeste appeared at the top of the stairs still in her nightdress. She stood looking down, a hand on the railing. "Do you want me to turn it off, Odette? I'll turn it off if it bothers you."

"Not off, Celeste. Just down a little. Or close your door. It's awfully loud."

"I'm sorry, Odette."

"Don't worry about it. Just close your door. And maybe you should get dressed. It's nearly ten o'clock."

"Okay, I'll do that."

How her sister loved those old Disney cartoons. Even now, at eighty, she never tired of laughing at the nonsense of those animated figures on the screen. When Raoul was here, he joined her in laughing at them. Jesus, Joseph, and Mary, the two of them in stockinged feet sitting at the foot of the bed. At the kitchen table she finished her second cup of coffee and rinsed and dried the cup. It was two weeks since she got rid of him, but Raoul's presence in the house still lingered. Unnerving really. She should never have agreed to it. A regrettable moment of weakness. A serious mistake. He wasn't in the place five minutes before he began to go on about what a fine big house it was and with so much room. And what a classy neighbourhood! In no time at all he was acting as if he belonged there. Yes, a serious mistake, and it had cost her money to get rid of him. Not that she was worried about money anymore. But she still hated throwing it away on the likes of Raoul Cloutier.

Today James Hillyer would be arriving by train and staying at the Chateau Frontenac. She couldn't remember now whether or not he said he would telephone. But she could remember that they had agreed to have dinner tomorrow at the big hotel. Quite remarkable, really, to receive that phone call from Danielle about a man in Toronto who was looking for her after all those years. Danielle said that he'd placed notices in the Montreal papers asking for information on the whereabouts of Odette Huard. Danielle had sent her the clipping. It was the first time she had seen her name in a newspaper. Then he had phoned her, a retired professor of something or other. English poetry? Something like that. But she could remember him now, a rather clumsy boy with blond hair, a friend of the boy in the wheelchair. Or was he a friend? She seemed to remember some friction between them. Anyway, it didn't matter. He had invited her to dinner and it was fairly certain that such a man would have a good pension from the university and not be interested in her money.

Even now, after nearly five months, she was still entranced by the big house and everything in it: the gleaming white stove and refrigerator in her kitchen. The dishwasher. Not in her most fanciful dreams had she ever imagined owning a dishwasher. Sometimes, like today, she enjoyed just walking through the rooms of her house looking at what she now possessed: the sofa and chairs and end tables in the living room, the china cabinet in the dining room, the beds and dressers upstairs. Or she just liked to stand by the front door looking out at the big verandah and the flower garden across the street and beyond that to the green expanse of the Parc des Champs-de-Bataille. That old fool Raoul was certainly right about one thing. It was a classy neighbourhood, and she was glad she had bought a house on this street. Her sisters, of course, thought she was being extravagant. Showing off, Lucille said. Well maybe, but so what? Yes, it was expensive and she could still remember her hand trembling as she signed the cheque and handed it to the pleasant woman at the real estate office. And again when she signed another at the furniture store. An enormous sum. But why should she have felt nervous about signing those cheques? They had plenty of money left in the bank, secured in guaranteed investment certificates. More than enough to last them for the rest of their lives. People who say that money cannot buy happiness have never been poor. They have never grown up in cold-water flats with outside staircases. They have never worried about the rent money on the first day of the month, the rising tension as the day approached and you counted what you had left in your purse. Everything down to the last dime.

Oddly enough, she still worried from time to time that she would somehow lose it all. It was as though she didn't feel entitled to be this well off, she and Celeste, living in this lovely house. A pair of women from St. Henri. As if Celeste cared. She was happy enough as long as she had her cartoons, her ice cream treat in the afternoon, and her daily bottle of beer before dinner. She had been happy enough living with Odette in St. Henri after Odette rescued her from that dismal place run by the Holy Sisters, with its grey walls and innumerable crucifixes, its smell of unwashed bodies and urine, and the damp, unfriendly looks from the lay nurses. That is where Sylvie and Lucille had put her.

When she visited the place that Sunday afternoon ten years ago, she was appalled: in the small room shared by four women, Celeste was sitting on the edge of her bed staring into space. The three other women were looking vacantly at a blaring television. When Celeste saw her, she began to weep and soon buried her head in Odette's chest. Four old women cooped up in that tiny room. One of them, she learned, had an awful tongue on her and regularly bullied Celeste. That Sunday afternoon she had gone straight to the Mother Superior's office and told her that she was taking her sister home. Celeste was not happy in this place, she said. The Mother Superior had only three words that finally emerged from those thin lips. "Please yourself, madame."

They took a taxi to her place on rue Marchand. The flat wasn't very big but there was room enough for two, and Celeste was so happy it was worth it just to look at her. Poor Celeste, damaged from birth and in that awful place. Odette couldn't

get over it, and when her sister called, outraged by what she had
done, she had given Sylvie an earful. That was long before the
lottery win. She was working then at her last job at Dubé Taxi,
as a dispatcher directing drivers to their various destinations in
the city. It paid enough to keep them warm and dry and fed with
not much left over. She knew her sisters would never forgive
her, but then they had never forgotten her troubles with men
and her shady past, as they called it. What did she care? They had
always stuck together, Sylvie and Lucille; even as kids they had
resented her for ordering them around, playing the older sister.
She was just happy to have Celeste with her. Celeste kept that
apartment spotless while Odette worked. And each Friday (her
lucky day, she said) Celeste went to the *dépanneur* on the corner
to buy ice cream and her lottery ticket. All those years of buying
tickets. And then last November their lives changed. In a way it
was quite funny. All her life she had no time for lotteries. As far
as she was concerned, the odds on winning were ridiculous. It
was like throwing a five-dollar bill in the garbage every Friday.
But she never said any of that to Celeste. Why spoil it for her?
Her one indulgence from her old-age pension was buying that
weekly lottery ticket. But that week Celeste was ill with flu and
so Odette bought the ticket. The only one she had ever bought.
And it won. So, unbelievable good fortune was handed to them
a week later when the winning tickets were announced on the
local radio station.

But winning all that money also brought problems. At first
her sisters were honey-tongued with congratulations and good
wishes. Then there were not so subtle suggestions that perhaps
in view of the fact that she was now quite rich, Odette might
like to share the wealth with various members of the family.

There were nephews and nieces who were struggling, and why couldn't Aunty Odette help out a little? Or in some cases a lot. Was it any wonder she was glad to get out of Montreal and start again with Celeste in Quebec City? As for the rest of them, they could go to hell. They had always condemned her for the life she led. So let them think what they like. She wasn't interested in helping any of them except perhaps Sylvie's daughter Danielle, the only niece she could tolerate, and even then Danielle's big mouth bothered her. But at least she had never asked for money. She was independent, the best of the bunch. By moving to Quebec City, Odette thought she might be free of them all. And then she got a phone call from Raoul's sister, Monique La-Croix. This was the first of many calls. Monique lived in Sainte Foy, a suburb of the city, with her husband, Bertrand, who was now retired after twenty-five years in the civil service. When she and Raoul were living together forty years ago, she didn't mind Monique and Bertrand. They all lived in Montreal then, and sometimes she and Raoul would go for Sunday dinner. But Raoul wasn't comfortable with his sister's husband and always complained afterwards about Bertrand being stuck up. Odette didn't say so, but she thought that perhaps Bertrand LaCroix didn't particularly enjoy sharing a meal with a jailbird either. Still, those occasions had been pleasant enough and Monique had always treated Odette well. But after she and Raoul broke up for the last time, she lost touch with Monique until this phone call a month ago when Monique told her that Raoul had been living with them in Sainte Foy for a few weeks. He had been in Bordeaux Prison and then lived for a couple of years with a woman in Drummondville. They had met while the woman was visiting her brother, and when Raoul was released, she invited him into her home. On hearing this, Odette had shaken her head. Another gullible woman who thinks she can reform a man and puts up with him until she has had enough beating and bruising and so locks the door one day. From there Raoul moved in with his sister and her husband. Odette finally had to ask, "Why are you telling me all this, Monique? I'm no longer interested in your brother. That's over and done with. It's all in the past."

"But he talks about you all the time, Odette. 'Where is Odette?' he says. 'I want to see my wife.'"

"But I'm not his wife and never was. You know that."

"Maybe, but poor Raoul doesn't. He has that old people's disease now, Alzheimer's, and is often confused. It's affected his memory. We finally had to put him in a home for the elderly. But he's not happy there. Could you not just see him? Just a visit some afternoon? Bertrand and I could drive him to your place. Just see him for an hour or two? I know it would do him a world of good."

She finally gave in to Monique's pleading, and the following Sunday just over two weeks ago she had heard the heavy rapping on the front door and there he was. She saw him through the front-door window, and when she opened the door, he thrust a bouquet of wilting flowers at her. The flowers had to be Monique's work. She was sure of it. Raoul had never bought a flower in his life, so she imagined his sister was trying to make him more appealing. Even at eighty-two, his black hair was only flecked with grey. He had weathered a harsh and unforgiving life, his face well marked by time and old violence; she saw a sallowness there too from all that prison life over the years. God, he had been in and out of jail all his life. Now he was an elderly hulk of a man in a grey suit that was much too small for him, a suit that hadn't seen a dry cleaner's in who knew how long.

She could still remember the first time she had laid eyes on him. It was 1948 and she was nineteen. Her first day at the Green Mermaid on Highway 132 on the outskirts of Rivière du Loup. "The roadhouse" most local people called it, and she was there in the afternoon to be coached by two of the other strippers. In a room backstage they were showing her how to take her time. Pay attention to the music. She was a performer, so perform. One of the girls was a lanky blonde with a bossy attitude. Loraine or Elaine. Something like that. But she was a good teacher. "Make them wait," she said. And the other girl nodded in agreement. "They like to look you over and you're young, so they want to take their time looking at your tits and ass. As soon as you come out, they are already screwing you in their minds, so don't rush things. Tease them. Make their tongues hang out." The other girl had laughed. But Odette was only half listening. She had watched the girls the day before and figured she could do as well as they were doing. And she had practised in the motel. As they were talking to her that afternoon, she was staring across the room at the best-looking man she had ever seen. He had just come in a side door and he was looking at her too. Not smiling. As she would learn, smiling didn't come easily to Raoul Cloutier. He carried a perpetual scowl with him most days. But it only added to his good looks, suggesting at least that this was not a frivolous man. The blond stripper had noticed Odette's attention and smiled. "That's Raoul Cloutier. One of the bouncers. A good-looking guy, isn't he? He's screwed all of us, honey, and you'll get your turn, but be warned. Use some Vaseline. He's got an awful cock on him."

In the hallway two weeks ago she had taken the flowers from him. He just seemed embarrassed to be seen holding them. When she had opened the front door to look for the car that had brought him, she saw Monique waving to her from the passenger side. "Hi, Odette," she called. That silly grin pasted on her face. "Bertrand and I have some chores to do. We'll be back to pick him up about four o'clock, okay?" Chores to do on a Sunday when many of the stores were closed? She had to wonder about that as she watched the car disappear down the street. Celeste was happy to see Raoul, and he picked her up and whirled her around.

"Easy now, Raoul," Odette cried. "Be careful, she's frail."

Raoul only shrugged. "My little Celeste. How are you?" Celeste only giggled. She'd always had a crush on Raoul. Harmless infatuation. And to his credit Raoul had always treated her like a little sister. Perhaps her childlike nature presented no threat to him. Odette didn't really understand the affection between them. And it was genuine affection. The two of them just seemed to enjoy one another's company, though Celeste said very little.

Raoul was then inspecting her house, wandering from room to room. "Nice place you got here," he said. "This must have cost you something, Odette."

"Yes, it was not cheap, that's for sure." She was glad he didn't ask how much. She would have had to lie.

As he listened, he shrugged again. "Lucky you, Odette."

And she sensed the resentment in his voice. "You're right. It was luck. Just pure luck. A row of numbers on a lottery ticket."

He looked puzzled for a moment and then followed Celeste up the staircase. She wanted to show him her room. Odette stayed in the kitchen wondering if she should offer him a beer. It was the hospitable thing to do and one wouldn't hurt. He seemed all right. Lucid enough. She'd give Celeste her daily beer too. They could enjoy their drinks together. She could use a drink herself; it only took a few minutes to feel that old familiar tension in her neck with Raoul in the house. What a long shadow he had cast over her life, and it was still there even now at her age. Standing at the kitchen counter, she poured some brandy into a glass and, after adding a little tap water, drank half of it. In the last few months she had grown fond of brandy. It was now her favourite drink. She felt the welcoming warmth flooding through her. She promised herself that she would survive Raoul's visit as long as he was reasonable. It was nearly two o'clock. But giving him beer worried her. As soon as she took the cap off one of the bottles, she began to fret. If he could stick to one beer it would be fine. She had seen him drink a dozen bottles in an afternoon and walk away. But he could also turn ugly with drink. Before she could pour the beer into the sink, Raoul and Celeste came into the kitchen and it was too late, so she gave them the beer.

"It's early, Celeste, but you can have yours now with Raoul."

Her sister smiled. "Good, good. Thank you, Odette."

Raoul took his beer without a word. He seemed to be sulking now and she wondered if these shifts in mood had anything to do with this Alzheimer's disease. But then he had always been a moody man.

They sat around the kitchen table, the three of them. She had wanted to sit in the living room. Was that just vanity? Showing off her expensive furniture? Make him see how much he was missing? It didn't matter. He had come straight into the kitchen and sat down. Raoul came from the countryside and the kitchen was where you talked. Why would it be any different in a house worth a million dollars? At least that was how she read his brooding face. Celeste had brought down a book of old photographs and was showing them to him. He looked at them as she turned the pages, but Odette sensed he was already bored. He wanted to set things straight. He had a reason for being there. And he began by looking up from that book of old pictures and asking when he could move in. A four-bedroom house. There was lots of room. If she didn't want to sleep with him, that was fine. He could use one of the two empty bedrooms.

"You could use a man around this place, Odette. To cut the grass and shovel the snow in winter. Fix things. I'm handy enough if I have the tools. But you can buy me some with all your money." He didn't offer any assurance that he would change his ways. No apologies for the times he had treated her so badly. He seemed to feel he had a right to live in her house. And he was clearly puzzled and angry at why he even had to ask. "You are my wife, Odette. A husband and wife should live together in their old age. You've had some luck. I haven't. But now we can be together again. It's a good arrangement. And we have Celeste with us. We'll look after one another."

As she listened, she was also watching the minute hand on the kitchen clock. It was so like Raoul to ignore all the causes of his problems. He never asked himself why he had spent so much time in prison. In Bordeaux. In Donnacona, where they put him away for three years for nearly killing a man with his fists. She felt herself getting more and more angry. A growing fury within as she thought of Monique and Bertrand dropping him off on a Sunday and not even coming into the house to say hello. Was she now expected to be Raoul's babysitter? She finished her drink in one gulp. "What are you drinking there?" he asked.

"It's brandy, Raoul. Courvoisier."

The name meant nothing to him and she wondered why she had mentioned it.

"That's a pretty fancy drink for a woman like you."

"A woman like me, Raoul? What does that mean?"

He shrugged. "Well, you know your background, my girl. Like me you came from ordinary people. Living in St. Henri and all that. Beer was plenty good enough for you in those days."

How she had wanted to say, "Fuck you, Raoul. Get out of my house." But she couldn't. It would be throwing gasoline on a bonfire. She had to put up with him until the LaCroixs returned, and then they could have him back with interest. So she said nothing but left the kitchen and went upstairs. A few moments later she heard the murmuring voices and then Celeste giggling. When she went back down, she had cooled off and sat at the kitchen table mustering as much patience as she could manage while he talked about the place his sister had put him in. How much he hated it. And it wasn't fair and it wasn't right for Odette to leave him there. He was sharing a room with a man he couldn't stand. He described him as a stupid fucker who just wanted to watch those game shows all day and night.

"Ah, Raoul," Odette said, "that must be a terrible hardship for you." But her sarcasm didn't register.

"And the people who run the place," he said, "always harping on something. Don't do this. Don't do that. It's worse than Bordeaux."

"Yes, yes, I can see how that must be terrible," she said,

glancing up again at the clock. How long could she put up with his whining?

That afternoon, however, things got worse. When Monique and Bertrand returned, they stayed in the car for perhaps five minutes, hoping, she supposed, that she would bring Raoul out to them. But he was in no humour to leave and she wanted them to see how obstinate he could be sitting at the kitchen table. And after five minutes they did come to the door and Celeste let them in. When Monique told Raoul it was time to go, he bellowed. "I am not going. I belong here, goddamn it." Odette noticed how Bertrand LaCroix flinched at the fury in Raoul's voice and Celeste began to cry. Then Monique was kneeling by her brother's chair, whispering urgently to him. But Odette could hear only the word *please* being repeated over and over again. "I belong with my wife here in this house," he kept saying. "We are a family with Celeste."

That was when Odette said calmly, "I'm calling the police."

Monique shook her head. "No, no, don't do that, Odette. There'll be a terrible scene."

"He's making a scene now," she said. "They'll know what to do with him."

Monique got to her feet and whispered to Odette. "Give me a few more minutes with him."

So she went upstairs to calm down but already she had an idea, a possible way to get him out of the house without involving the police and alerting the neighbourhood. Opening the bottom drawer of her dresser, she counted out thirty ten-dollar bills from the cache she always thought of as emergency money. Uneasy with the credit card the man at the bank had given her, she still liked cash. It was familiar and she enjoyed having some on hand in case she needed it. She was also skeptical of ATMs. What an old-fashioned person I now am, she thought, as she recounted the bills. Three hundred dollars. The money would tempt him. Money was always important to Raoul and he never had much of it. When he did steal it, he never kept it for long. She imagined that he was virtually penniless, his old age-pension eaten up by the residence fee. All those ten-dollar bills would look like a small fortune and perhaps take his mind off staying in her house. Or so she thought as she came into the kitchen and laid out the money in front of him.

He looked at it with dull eyes. "What's this?"

"Take it, Raoul. A little present. But if you take it, you must leave." He hesitated. She knew he wouldn't like the idea of being bought off. But there on the kitchen table was the price of his leaving and it must have looked like a great deal of money. It could buy a lot of beer and whatever else he might feel the need for. A woman off the street perhaps. To take to some room. If he was still interested in all that. She watched him pick up the money and fold it into a shirt pocket beneath his suit coat.

She then took Monique aside and told her that she would make up the difference each month for a private room in that retirement home. Maybe that would make him a little happier there. She was disappointed that Monique didn't seem as grateful as she might have been. Still it got them out of the house so that she could make dinner for Celeste and enjoy another brandy while working in the kitchen. It bothered her a little, giving away all that money and committing herself to helping with Raoul's care, and she now regretted her generosity. And no doubt one day he would be back knocking on her door.

That night, quite late, she phoned James Hillyer and told

him to postpone his visit for a couple of weeks. She could hear the disappointment in his voice, but he had gone along with it, and now she was ready to enjoy a dinner with James at the Chateau Frontenac. First, though, a bath with another glass of brandy.

That had been a jarring Sunday afternoon weeks ago. She used to know how to handle Raoul better. Over the years she had learned how to avoid his tantrums. At least sometimes. Now it seemed that she had forgotten or could no longer be bothered. Yet a part of her pitied him. Raoul Cloutier was only the husk of the man she used to know. And with that disease, she guessed his mind and memory would one day be entirely gone.

Raoul

What *day of the week* was it anyway? Not that it mattered, he supposed. One day was as good or as bad as another. But how many days ago had he been in that big house? Christ, what a place! A mansion. And Odette owned it. The girl he married when she was just a kid from St. Henri who used to take off her clothes in front of men for money. Now acting all high and mighty. Paying him off to stay away, goddamn it. His own wife, who drank brandy. Beer wasn't good enough for her. What was the name of that street she lives on? There was some kind of park across the road. He could remember that. But where the fuck was it in this city? Looking around, he raised his finger for the waiter, who was on the other side of the room talking to some men. The waiter nodded at him but he didn't come right over. Annoying. At

the table next to him a loudmouth. Both his arms tattooed, for
Christ's sake. A red bandana on his head. Trying to look tough.
He was younger than the other men. Shooting his mouth off
about some big shot friend of his. Pure bullshit and an irritating
presence in the mostly empty bar. He felt a growing thickness
in his chest. He wanted another beer and he wished the waiter
would stop talking and laughing and look over his way again. At
the table next to him the tattooed young guy continued to yap.
It was all very annoying.

When he was in Donnacona, the shrink told him that when
he felt upset about things or people, he should breathe in deeply
and hold his breath for four seconds and then exhale. Do that
a few times and you'll feel better; you'll calm down, the shrink
said. An old guy with greying hair and bad breath. What he said
sounded like bullshit, but in fact most of the time it worked. It
slowed you down and you focused. That was the word he used.
You focused on the breathing and forgot the agitation. Yes, that
was another word he used a lot. He used to practise in bed when
his cellmate in the bunk below was getting on his nerves. He
would lie there listening to the man muttering to himself in
the middle of the night. Jabbering on about how he was going
to do this to someone. Do that to somebody else. That was all
bullshit and it was irritating. He often felt like jumping down
and pulling the guy to his feet and just clocking him. But that
would mean two or three months in close confinement. Only
one hour a day in the exercise yard and twenty-three hours by
yourself. He learned all that over the years. So it wasn't worth it.

Now, however, he just wanted a beer. And again he raised
his finger and the waiter nodded and went to the bar. Raoul
pulled a rumpled ten-dollar bill from his pocket. How many

did he have left? Odette had given him thirty. That was three hundred dollars. A damned insult. Buying him off like that. She and Monique and that wimp, Bertrand, sweet-talking him into leaving the big house on that street with the park across the road. Odette just laying out all that money in front of him on the kitchen table. He shouldn't have taken it. He might still be there. In his own bedroom. Where he deserved to be. That was a Sunday afternoon two or three weeks ago, maybe. And they put him back in that fucking place where they treat you like a little kid. Well, he was going back to Odette's house and demand—yes, demand—to be let in where he belonged. They were man and wife, for Christ's sake. He thought he had maybe four or five ten-dollar bills left and a pocketful of change, which he now put on the table, stacking the coins into little castles of dimes, quarters, and nickels. He began to count the coins but he soon lost track of things. That too was annoying. He used to be good at arithmetic. It was the only thing in school he liked and he was the best in the sixth grade, his last year. He was only eleven, but his father needed him on the farm. Now he couldn't count worth shit. Numbers just confused him. He figured there was enough change there for another beer and then he'd leave.

What did Odette say to him that Sunday? "I don't want to live with you anymore, Raoul. Monique is going to get you a room of your own in the residence and I will help your sister with the price of that. You'll be well looked after there." Everybody was treating him like a kid, and now with all her money, Odette was acting like a big shot. There was plenty of room in that house for him, and he deserved to be there. Yes, acting like a big shot. A little stripper who got lucky. He should never have let them talk him into leaving that day. It wasn't right. They

were man and wife and that house was as much his as it was
hers. A man and a wife had to share things. It was the law. He
thought somebody once told him that.

When the waiter came by with the beer, Raoul pointed to
the pile of coins. "Take it out of that," he said, adding, "and will
you tell the guys at the next table to pipe down. Especially the
guy with the tattooed arms. I can't think straight for his yap-
ping."

The waiter shrugged as he picked through the coins. When
he finished, he went over to the noisy table and spoke to the tattooed man, who looked around the waiter and smiled at Raoul.
Then he gave him a little wave that said it all. He might as well
have said, "Fuck you, old man." Raoul looked away. No use getting upset over assholes. He had nearly finished the second beer
but wouldn't leave just yet because it would seem too much like
he was being chased out. Picking up the few coins left from the
piles, he sensed an old familiar stirring within. An excitement of
sorts. There might be trouble coming soon and was he up for
it? Taking the ten-dollar bills out of his jacket, he counted them
carefully again. Five. That was fifty dollars. It had to last him
until his pension cheque at the end of the month. He had been
on his own a long time now. Most of his life, when he thought
about it. Since he was sixteen and left the farm. Thinking about
it took his mind off the smirk on that tattooed fucker's mug.

He was thinking now about that long-ago day with his father
and mother in the kitchen. What year was that? The German
war was on. His oldest brother, Louis, had run off to Montreal
to join the army. But Louis was in his twenties then. The other
brothers and sisters stayed on the farm. But where were they
that Saturday morning? Out in the barn maybe. It was spring.

April or May. The fields were all green. He could remember that. When he came down the stairs into the kitchen, his father was shouting at his mother. She had done something he didn't like. Who knows what? She was always taking shit from the old bastard. And she was pregnant again. She had told Raoul months before that she hoped this child would be her last. She must have been in her early forties then. And she was big in the belly that spring day. Only a few weeks before the doctor would come and get that baby out of her. And that would be his sister, Monique. Now somewhere in her sixties.

It was funny in a peculiar way to think of Monique now in her sixties being inside her mother on that day when he had a fight with his father. Coming into the kitchen, he had seen the second blow, with his mother falling backwards into the rocking chair by the kitchen stove, crying with her hands across her eyes, the tears leaking through her fingers, moaning, "No, Jean. No more, for the love of God."

He had been a good size at sixteen. Nearly as tall as his father though not as heavy. Not an inch of fat on him. And he had fought with his brothers from time to time. They were a quarrelsome family, the Cloutiers. Everybody in the township knew that. Sometimes he surprised his older brothers by holding them down with one hand at their throats. But that day he might have been yelling to his father to leave his mother alone. He was no longer certain but probably he was yelling. But he can remember his father's bad temper. Raoul had pulled him away from his mother in the rocking chair, and when the old man looked at him, his face was red with hatred and rage. "What? What?" he kept saying. "You are telling me what to do in my own house?" That was when he hit his father.

In a fight surprise is everything. He had learned that in the village schoolyard and in the barn with his brothers. So while his father was sputtering with anger, he struck him with a good right hand flush on the nose and he watched the blood spilling onto the checkered shirt and the wide grey suspenders. He had stepped back then, expecting his father's charge, an enraged bull with those big hands twisting him down into a headlock where his face would be punched over and over. As a child he saw Louis absorb such a beating and his nose was never quite right again. But when his father's charge came that day, he had stepped aside, the big fist just brushing his face. And when his father turned again towards him, Raoul struck a blow that sent the old man reeling backwards, where he hit his head on the edge of the wood stove, his eyes fluttering as he sank to the floor. His mother was crying from the rocking chair. "Dear God, you've killed him, Raoul. You've killed your father." She was crossing herself as she said the words. And for a few minutes, he thought he had. His father lay still on the floor and his mother, after getting up with difficulty because of her big stomach, was kneeling by her husband and praying, "Please God, don't let him die." His mother was sitting on the floor in front of the stove holding her husband. Now and then she joined her hands in prayer. "Mary, Mother of God, don't let him die." She sat there weeping with a face bruised from blows but praying for her husband's life in front of that old stove with the word *Commandeur* on the oven door. Now isn't that a funny thing? The fact that he can remember the name of a stove from over sixty years ago, but now half the time he can't remember lots of things. Things he should know. Not even the name of that place Monique and Bertrand put him into. Sometimes he

wakes up and for five minutes has no idea where he is. Or what
her name is. The nurse who comes around to see how he's
doing. But he can remember the name of that old stove and the
day he fought with his father. Beat him too. And the old man
didn't die. He can remember him opening his eyes a little and
pushing at his wife to leave him alone. Raoul went up to his
room then and stuffed some clothes into an old cardboard suitcase that once belonged to somebody. His grandfather, maybe.
There was no future for him now on the farm. When he went
down to the kitchen again, his father was still on the floor rub-
bing his head slowly like a man waking up with a hangover.
Raoul told his mother that he was leaving. He held up the old
suitcase to show her he meant business. He'd get a job in Montreal, he said, and promised he'd write. She nodded. Told him
not to join the army. "Don't fight in the English war," she said.
But he told her not to worry. He was too young. He walked
away from it all then. Yes. Walked all the way to the village and
the highway, where he hitchhiked to Montreal. With that war
on there was work in the city if you were young and strong. At
first he got a job in a junkyard owned by a Jewish guy. Taking apart old cars. Then he worked in construction. Lived in a
boarding house in St. Henri. For a kid he did okay in Montreal.
He didn't go back to the farm for how long? Must have been
seven or eight years. By then he was at the Green Mermaid.
Had his own car. A 1940 Ford coupe. He came back to the farm
looking sharp in a double-breasted suit with white-and-brown
shoes. When he went into the house, he saw his father in the
rocking chair by the stove. A strange smile on him. He looked
shriveled, old, and weak. When he hugged his mother, she told
him that something had happened in his father's chest. A heart

attack maybe or a strike. No, not a strike. A stroke. He'd had this stroke and was good for nothing now. And that was true. His father didn't even recognize him but smiled when they shook hands.

It was summer and when he went outside, his brothers and sisters were standing around admiring his car. Some of them were married by then. To him they all looked poor. None of them had travelled more than twenty miles from the farm. He was glad he'd left home. "What a nice car, Raoul. You've made something of yourself, I bet." Yes, he'd done okay. No point in telling them about his time in Bordeaux. He had assaulted a guy outside a tavern. A bum rap. The guy had started the fight. But they didn't need to know that. Monique was there that day. She was only a little girl with pigtails. Maybe eight or nine. The baby of the family. He took her for a ride in the Ford. On the way back along the country road he let her steer the car, sitting on his lap. When they came into the farmyard, his family cheered. They were happy for him. "Have you got a girlfriend, Raoul?"

Sure he had a girlfriend. She was pretty too. "An actress," he said.

"An actress? Now that's something. What's her name?"

"Odette. Odette Huard."

They asked him about his job at the roadhouse and he told them what he did. He made two fists and held them up so they could see his bruised knuckles. "Sometimes," he said, "we get customers who think they're tough. So I have to use these."

"I'll bet you've never lost a fight, Raoul."

"Never," he said. "I can't afford to lose. If it got around that I'd lost a fight, I wouldn't be worth anything to the owner."

"You should get into wrestling, Raoul. Like Yvon Robert. He never loses a fight. I read about him in a magazine. He's a millionaire now."

"I might do that one day," he said. "Maybe I'll fight Yvon Robert." And they laughed.

Before he left that day, he went back in the house and said goodbye to his mother and father. It was the last time he saw the old man alive. When he died a few years later, Raoul showed up at the funeral at the village church. Odette came with him into the countryside in the '40 Ford. It was just before they got married. Or was it after they got married? He was no longer sure. They had both left their jobs at the Green Mermaid. Odette said she was tired of taking off her clothes in front of men with their hands down their pants. She told him it was degrading. He didn't know what the word meant and that annoyed him. The saucy little bitch was starting to use fancy words around him and he didn't like it. Who did she think she was anyway?

He called her Miss Fancy Pants. Throwing around big words like that. She told him she would talk any way she pleased. He didn't own her. He cuffed her for that. It was maybe the first time. He wasn't sure, but he did cuff her and they split for a while. That was when she started to work for that taxi company, taking calls over the telephone and telling the drivers where to go. Dubé Taxi. That was the name and he felt good about remembering it. Yes, that was when he decided to try his hand at wrestling. He went to a gym on rue Ste. Catherine and asked a guy named Lenny or Larry. An Anglais, but he spoke French too. He asked this Lenny for lessons and paid ten dollars a lesson. He told the guy he wanted to be like Yvon Robert, the best wrestler in Quebec. Lenny had shrugged. "We'll see. You got a good build on you. But something tells me you'd be better playing the villain."

Villain? What was a villain? he asked, and Lenny asked him if he'd ever seen an actual wrestling match. Sure he'd seen them. He'd been to the Forum a few times on Monday nights. He'd seen Yvon Robert in the ring. A good wrestler. He almost never lost. "Well," Lenny said, "Yvon is one of the good guys. First thing is, he's good-looking. But he's also a nice guy. People like him. They cheer for him. They never like the guy he's fighting because that guy is the villain. And I think you'd do better as a villain."

"What the fuck is this villain business? I don't get it."

"The villain is the bad guy, Raoul. He might win, but if he does, it's through some dirty move. The villain cheats and has to be mean. Don't take offence but with those dark eyes and looks of yours, you're better fitted for the role of villain. You can make a lot of money as the bad guy."

"What's all this good guy, bad guy stuff? I don't get it."

Lenny then told him that professional wrestling wasn't real fighting. "It's a show, Raoul," he said. "An exhibition. You throw a guy around. Do some moves on him. And then he does the same to you. It's like two actors in a play."

"Actors in a play? You mean the fighting isn't real?"

The guy laughed. "Jesus, Raoul, how long ago did you leave the farm? Wrestling isn't like professional boxing. In wrestling the fix is in all the time. The guys take turns winning. It's all worked out. You build your reputation around showmanship."

And what was that? he asked.

"Showmanship," said Lenny. "Well, it's how well you can

jack up the crowd. Either to like you if you're the good guy, or hate you if you're the villain. It's like acting, Raoul."

"Acting," he said. "Christ."

"So you have to have a gimmick." *Gimmick.* Another word he'd never heard of.

Lenny then opened a locker door and fished out a black cape and brought it over to him. "Try this on. You're not a bad-looking guy and you got this kind of darkness in your looks."

"What's that mean?"

"It suggests you're a really mean son of a bitch who won't be afraid to use a few dirty tricks to beat the other guy. But your dark looks may win you some fans, particularly the ladies. They like cheering for a big dangerous-looking guy. It drives their boyfriends and husbands crazy when women are cheering for you."

Raoul tried on the cape and looked in the mirror. For a moment he thought he looked foolish, but maybe not.

"We'll put long black pants on you. Looks more sinister," Lenny said.

Sinister? What did that mean? But he was getting some idea. "I've got it," Lenny said. "We'll call you Captain Darkness or something like that. I can see you coming down the aisle with the crowds gawking at you. We'll have to teach you how to swagger. You're full of yourself and you show it. People hate that kind of overconfidence because none of those schmucks have anything like it. So they want to hate you because you got so much. Meantime their wives and sweethearts are eyeballing you. That night you might lose but you're a bad loser and make a fuss about it. The crowd won't like that but you have to show them that basically you don't give a shit what they like or don't like. You're Captain Darkness." Then he added, "Yes something like that. I think it might work. But remember, you're always acting, Raoul. Wrestling is performance art."

Performance art? Acting? Showmanship. Gimmick. Captain Fucking Darkness in long black pants and a cape. And none of it was real fighting. He couldn't believe he'd been so stupid all those years, and his face must have said as much because Lenny then said, "Christ, Raoul, if these two-hundred-and-fifty-pound men were really fighting, we'd have a funeral on our hands every other week. It's just entertainment. It's as simple as that. Now let's practise some of those moves we've been working on." But after that day he never went back.

The next week he got a job as a longshoreman unloading freighters. Just before Christmas that year he and Odette were invited to a party at the taxi garage. He was already suspicious of the owner, Marcel Dubé. By then he had persuaded Odette to move back in with him. Dubé was in his late thirties or early forties then. A former boxer, a middleweight, and he was still a good-looking guy. Smartly dressed at that party, where he and Odette seemed to talk to each other all night. They seemed awfully chummy to him. She was always talking about how nice he was to work for, and one night a week before or after that party he had enough of this talk about the perfect boss, and after a long silence at the table he said, "I'm asking you and I want the truth, Odette. Are you fucking this boss of yours?"

She had frowned at him. "No, I'm not, and don't be so vulgar."

There was another word she had come up with lately. *Vulgar*. She used it on him when he swore or farted or did a lot of things he'd always done. Vulgar. Well, he knew what the word meant and so what? But maybe she got that job because the guy knew she would put out for him. He went on to say, "If I find out that you're fucking Mr. Nice Boss, I'll give you the beating of your life. And then I'll go to Dubé and give the hotshot some of the same."

And she said, "If you lay a hand on me, I'll be out of here in a minute and I'll not want to see you again. I hope you understand that."

Then she got up from the table and crossed the kitchen to the hallway and he heard the slamming of the bathroom door. A week later at that Christmas party in the taxi garage he had watched her talking and laughing with Marcel Dubé while he stood apart or wandered off alone. He didn't know anyone there and he felt out of place. He always did at parties. He didn't know what to say to people or how to tell jokes. Was that his fault? He didn't think so. People are different. That night he walked to the back of the big garage away from others, slipping between parked taxis and cars under repair. In one corner of the garage he looked through the open venetian blinds of an office door. He guessed it was Marcel Dubé's office. He could see a desk and swivel chair. A girly calendar and a city map were pinned to the wall behind the desk. But what interested him more was the green couch in the room. And he can remember wondering what you would need a couch in an office for unless it was where you could close the blinds and shag an employee like Odette. He could picture her on that couch riding the owner of the taxi company late at night. When she worked the night shift, she didn't get home until two in the morning, and when she got into bed she often smelled of soap or perfume. As if she might have taken a shower to wash away the smell of sex. And she was never interested in him on those late nights.

She would say, "I'm tired Raoul, all right? I've been working for twelve hours." Yeah, right, he thought. And do you drink on the job too? Because sometimes he smelled liquor on her breath. How many of those hours were spent drinking and screwing on that green couch? Yet she was touchy when he questioned her. He often felt like hitting her, but he didn't because he was afraid he would lose her.

A few weeks after Christmas he was picked up by the cops. He and another guy had been helping themselves to some liquor they were unloading and selling it. Somebody squealed. He was soon back in Bordeaux for the next year.

Now the waiter came by and asked him if he wanted another beer and he shook his head. The men at the next table were laughing, making fun of somebody, maybe him for all he knew. So he asked the waiter again if he would tell them to pipe down because they were giving him a headache with their noise. This wasn't true. He didn't get headaches. He didn't think he'd ever had a headache in his life. But it sounded like a good reason for telling him.

But the waiter only frowned this time and said, "They have a right to enjoy themselves, sir. They are not doing any harm. If they bother you, perhaps you should find another place to drink."

After he left, Raoul wondered if the men at the next table had overheard the waiter, because the tattooed man with the red bandana waved again and said, "Are we bothering you, old fella? Are you trying to read your prayer book?" Raoul got up then and put on his jacket. With one hand he swept up the scattered coins into his other hand. As he passed the men, he stopped and the tattooed fellow smiled up at him and said, "Would you like to join us, Grandpa?"

Even at his age, Raoul was not slow with his hands, those big hands that had protected him in all his years. And so the tattooed man and his friends were startled when Raoul's left hand reached out swiftly and seized the man by the throat, lifting him to his feet. Raoul ignored the sound of an overturned chair and a man's hand on his back. "Hey now, mister. Take it easy. He's only joking."

Raoul said to the tattooed man, "I don't like to be mocked by a little shit like you. You shouldn't talk so loud, because you have nothing to say." And after he released the grip on the throat, the man fell back into his chair coughing and holding his neck. By then Raoul had turned and walked to the door. He didn't think the men at the table would follow him. They were ordinary workingmen who didn't want to get involved in violence. Most people didn't want to get involved in violence. He, on the other hand, didn't mind it at all.

When he stepped outdoors, it had stopped raining and behind the clouds now was a pale sun. The heavy warm air engulfed him as he walked towards Terrasse Dufferin, where he liked to lean against the railing and look down at the river. Many others, he noticed, also enjoyed staring down at the water, and he often wondered what it would be like to be on a ship heading out to sea. Where would that take him? To what countries across the sea? Again he had lost track of time and he no longer had a watch. He may have lost it or more likely it was stolen. A good deal of stealing went on in that place that Monique and Bertrand had put him in. He had told the woman at the desk that he was going for a walk, but that was morning and now it was afternoon. He had said he'd be back for lunch, but lunch would be finished now. They were probably glad to be rid of him for the day. He knew the nurses and cleaning people didn't like him, and he didn't know how to make them like him. The cleaning people would be in his room now looking through his things. Perhaps one of them stole his watch. One of the Negro women, maybe. She might have taken it to give to her boyfriend or husband. She was nice to him, but maybe that was all an act. The best thing that could happen would be to move out of that place and live with Odette in the big house. He didn't mind Odette's sister. She was slow at understanding things. Like a little kid, but she liked him.

Looking out at the river, he imagined himself with Odette on one of those big ships that took people on holidays to Florida or those islands down south. He would speak to Odette about that. They could plan a trip together and take along Celeste too. She would enjoy it. Odette could afford a holiday like that. Someone—perhaps it was his sister, Monique—told him that Odette was now worth millions after that lottery win. Leaning on the railing, he wondered how he had got into the city that morning and then he remembered that he'd taken a bus. Yes, he had left the residence and there was a bus stop half a block away and he had sat on the bus until he got to rue St. Louis and then had walked into the tavern for a beer. And now he was looking out at the river. The St. Lawrence River. He had done it all by himself. He could still get around even if he did forget things now and then. But where was Odette's house? What street did she live on and what was the house number? When he sat in the back seat of Bertrand's car that Sunday, he had not paid enough attention. If he had her address and house number, he could hail a taxi and have the fellow drive him there. It was as simple as that, and when he looked across the terrace to the little park, he noticed the phone booth. Her name would be in the phone book. He was glad he'd remembered to put his glasses in his shirt pocket, and in the phone booth he began to look for the number of Mrs. Raoul Cloutier. He wouldn't phone. He would surprise her by just showing up in a taxi. There were plenty of Cloutiers in the phone book, but no Mrs. Raoul Cloutier. As he turned the pages, he could remember his father and other men talking about the strongman Louis Cyr, who was once a cop in St. Henri. They talked of how Cyr put on exhibitions of his strength by pulling a locomotive with a leather cord in his teeth. Or tearing a phone book in half with his bare hands. By God, that must have taken some doing.

He wondered then if Odette had used her birth name. There were plenty of Huards in the phone book but he could not find an Odette Huard. If she did go by her birth name, it wasn't right. She was married to him. He could feel his anger growing. It was then that he noticed that he was gripping the phone book in both hands. Trying to rip it apart. And he must have been swearing, for when he looked up, he saw a woman who walked quickly past him after staring. She was now hurrying along the terrace talking into her ear phone. Or cell phone or whatever they call them. She must have been phoning the police, he thought, because only minutes later he looked up from the partly torn phone book to see two policemen staring at him, as if he were an animal in a cage. Behind them the revolving blue light of a police car. One of the cops was now rapping on the door. "What are you doing with the phone book, sir? Open the door." The other was trying to open it, but Raoul filled up the entire space and was wedged against the door. Again the cop said, "Open the door, sir." And Raoul slowly put the badly torn phone book back with its little chain and opened the door, and again the cop said, "What are you doing with that phone book, sir?" All he could think of saying was, "I can't find my wife's name in it."

James

In the dining room of the Chateau Frontenac, James was enjoying a large whisky while he awaited Odette's arrival. He was trying to remember the last time he and Odette had been together. Was it on that big iron bridge? Or was it in the cove beneath the bridge? It was all so long ago.

••

August 1944

When we reached the cove, we sat on our favourite log and looked out at the sea. She finally said, "My father is pretty nosy, isn't he?"

"That's all right," I said, "he's just curious about people. There's nothing wrong with that."

"Maybe not," she said. "Anyway, he says he's got a house for us. In St. Henri. Do you know Montreal, James?"

"No."

She was doing what she often did when we sat together on that log, leaning forward to scoop up a handful of sand, then letting it spill through her fingers.

"It's a poor part of the city," she said. "What do you say in English when the head is filled with lice?"

"It's lousy," I said.

"Yes, it's lousy. I've heard that word. And you use it to describe things that aren't good. So we're going to a lousy neighbourhood, but it's all he can afford, I guess."

I asked her when they would be leaving for Montreal.

"I don't know," she said. "Sometime next month. I'm not going to start school here, I know that. I'm going to stay on at the hotel until we leave. My father knows somebody who has a car and he is going up to Montreal to see about a job. My father thinks he can get him a job and so some of us can go up with him. The others will go with my mother on the train. I don't know what they'll do with our furniture. Send it by truck or something. When we get there, we'll be late for classes. Other kids will look at us and say things to each other. They'll laugh behind their hands. It's always the same."

She got up from the log, brushing the seat of her new slacks just the way her father had on the gallery steps. The afterglow from the sunset had left the sky a remarkably deep orange, and this was reflected in the water, which looked like a painting, only with the colour changing by the moment. Odette sat down again, but then got up. She couldn't keep still.

"When are you going home?" she asked.

"A week from Tuesday," I said. "The day after Labour Day."

"Gabriel is leaving next Saturday," she said over her shoulder as she walked down to the shore, where she began to skip stones across that coloured water. She threw the stones with a deft, sidearm motion, and I watched the little flashes of light in the darkening water. Then she turned and walked back towards me. How quickly the darkness had enfolded us. As she walked, I could no longer see her face clearly; she was only a figure in a white blouse and dark pants.

When she sat on the log beside me, she said, "Do you know what, James? I think I'm pregnant. I should have had the curse by now and anyway I feel funny."

"Funny?"

"Yes. Well, not funny in the way you think of the word, but different. I feel different. There's something going on inside me. My tits sometimes tingle." She leaned against me and took my arm. "Do you know about these things, James? About a girl's period and all that? The bees and the birds." She sounded almost amused, but I knew it was just an act.

"I'm sorry it's happened, Odette."

"Yes," she said, bending forward to pick up another handful of sand. "I am . . . how do you say it in English? I am in a pickle. I have always thought that is a funny way to describe something serious. To be in a pickle."

"Have you told him?" I asked.

She laughed. "Told Gabriel. No." Her no was so adamant, so scornful. As if I had suggested something ridiculous. "What can he do about it?" she said. "Marry me? Take me back with him to the States? A rich kid like that. Why should he care if I'm pregnant?"

"You're only sixteen, Odette," I said.

"Actually not," she said. "I won't be sixteen until December.

Two days before Christmas. But so what? Fifteen, sixteen, I'm still pregnant. I'm pretty sure of that now."

"You should tell him," I said. "He's responsible."

She laughed again and squeezed my arm. "You are such a proper guy, James. I like that about you. Maybe you should have been the one to make me pregnant, eh? You would look after me, I bet."

"Yes, I would look after you." I sounded so earnest, and it was easy enough to say, though I couldn't really imagine myself in such circumstances.

"Well," she said after a moment. "It wasn't all his fault. I didn't say no."

"You should tell him just the same," I said. "You should tell his mother too. They should help you out."

She was looking straight ahead, no longer holding my arm but hugging herself against the night air.

"They should, they should, they should. Who says they should, James? You? I can see me telling his mother. Sure I can. She'd love to hear the news, I bet."

"You have to tell them, Odette," I said. "It's not fair if they don't know."

She said nothing and we sat listening to the water lapping the shore. She then put her head on my shoulder. I could smell her hair and I listened to her murmur. "Merde, merde, merde."

"What are you going to do?" I asked. I liked the weight of her leaning against me.

"I don't know," she said dreamily, as if only half listening. "There are places to go. The Church has homes for people like me. The nuns look after you. I knew a girl once who went to one of these homes in Montreal."

"Have you told anyone else? Pauline?"

"No, she would just tell others. Pauline can't keep anything to herself. Piss on her. She will never know. I'll be gone from this *maudit* village by the time she finds out, if she ever does."

She was still talking as if half asleep, as if wearied by thinking of it all. Her head felt heavy on my shoulder, but I didn't care.

"You'll need money," I said. "Do you have any?"

"I have a little, yes."

"I can give you some," I said. "Maybe twenty-five dollars. I think I have that much."

She sat up and put her arm around me and kissed my neck.

"You are a nice boy, James," she said, "but I don't want your money."

"I want you to have it," I said. "I don't need it. I'm going home soon. My ticket is paid for."

"No," she said.

I felt such outrage then. None of it was fair. He was going to get away with it.

"I'm going to tell Gabriel if you won't," I said.

She pulled away from me at once.

"Don't do that," she said. "Don't mention this to him. It does no good. He's got enough to think about."

"Like what?"

"Like the life ahead of him," she said. "Gabriel is a spoiled boy, but there is good in him too. I had lots of fun with him. I should have been more careful. It's my fault too. I can't just blame him."

"He's a rich American show-off who cries like a baby when things don't go his own way. You saw him that day we had the picnic. Yelling like that."

Odette was shaking her head. "You are such a blamer, James. It's blame, blame, blame all the time. Why are you like that?

Gabriel can't help being the way he is. He's proud. I told you before. He didn't want to be carried like that. Like a child in the arms of that stupid bastard Emile, who just picked him up without a word. How would you like that to happen in front of your friends?"

I can't recall how I answered her question or even if I did. I can't even remember how that evening ended. We must have walked back from the cove together, but maybe not. Maybe I grew sulky over her loyalty to Gabriel and we returned by separate ways. We did that now and then after disagreeing, and that evening may have been one of those times. When I saw her the next day at the St. Lawrence Hotel, however, we were friends again. We smiled at each other in the hallway. I remember that.

• •

Hillyer had booked his room for five nights so that he now had until Saturday to explore Quebec and environs, hopefully with Odette. Perhaps it was the whisky but he felt buoyant and hopeful and wonderfully free. And if it came to that, he could take more time. He was under obligation to no one. He began to study the wine list, but when he glanced up, he could see the maître d' making his way through the tables followed by an elderly woman in a dark pantsuit and jacket. Even with the grey hair and lined face, he caught glimpses of the girl he had once known. She was smaller than he remembered, but so was he. Age shrinks us all, he thought, but so what? It didn't really matter. Nothing mattered now but seeing her. He felt almost giddy with happiness, as he stood up admiring the pearl necklace at her throat. "You look terrific, Odette."

"Thank you, James. You're not so bad yourself." And she

kissed him on both cheeks before sitting down. The waiter was grinning at both of them. "Two old folks now, eh?" Odette said. "But better here than you-know-where."

"Absolutely."

Odette looked up at the handsome waiter. Ever the flirt, she pointed at James. "*Soixante-deux ans*. Sixty-two years since we have seen one another." The waiter shook his head as if amazed and handed her the menu and complimented them both in French.

"They have a very good list here, Odette," James said. "A glass of something before dinner. Prosecco?"

"How about a glass of white wine?"

"Wonderful. Let's do that while we decide on dinner."

"Good idea," he said. "Sixty-two years. It's just so incredible to see you. Damn it, I think I'm still in love with you."

She laughed with delight. "Well, that's very nice to hear. But look at these prices. My goodness, it's expensive. We'll share the cost."

"Nonsense," he said. "It's my treat."

"There you are," she said. "Not five minutes after sixty-two years and already you're arguing with me."

Smiling he reached across the table and took her hand in both of his, a gesture so fundamentally unlike him that he felt a bit unnerved but at the same time immensely moved by her presence. Even after all those years. Astonishing.

"Yes, I was a stubborn boy and still am, I suppose. We disagreed on so many things. You thought I was a . . . ." He paused. "You had a favourite word to describe me. I was always complaining about things you said."

"Yes, and I was right, James. You did complain about a lot

of things. You didn't think much of your uncle who you were staying with in that house next to ours. You thought Gabriel was taking advantage of me. All the people over at that hotel in Percé were rich snobs. You never said what you liked, and yet there you were, living in a lovely part of this province. But nothing suited you. You didn't like the landlady in that house."

"Yes, you're right," he said, releasing her hand as the waiter brought the wine. "I am well rebuked. I was a fourteen-year-old cynic. That was me."

"The first one to remember that word I called you wins," she said, smiling at the waiter.

"And what does the winner get? "

"I don't know, we'll see."

He had ordered a bottle of Chablis. It was expensive but he didn't care. This was an occasion. He couldn't get over how happy he felt to see her. She had put on her glasses to read the menu. While the waiter was uncorking the wine, James suffered through the usual ritual of sniffing the cork and tasting the few drops in the glass, then looking up with an approving nod. When the waiter left, James said, "You look great, Odette."

Now she lowered the glasses and looked over them like a schoolteacher. "You already told me that, James."

"So what? It bears repeating. You've worn your years well."

She returned to the menu. "Thank you. It's a kind thing to say." She paused. "Coming as it does from an old sorehead."

"Of course," he said, and they both laughed.

"And since I won, James, I'm paying for the wine and no arguments."

"It's wickedly expensive," but she had already reached across the table and placed a finger on his lips.

"No more arguments. I can afford it. No doubt Danielle told you about the lottery win."

"Oh yes. Congratulations."

"Well, it's a mixed blessing winning all that money. It's wonderful never having to worry again about money because, believe you me, most of my life I've lived very close to the edge of poverty. I lived mostly from paycheque to paycheque. So it's wonderful not to have to worry about money anymore. Sometimes lying in bed at night I think I'm still dreaming and it never really happened." She smiled. "But of course it did. On the other hand, as they say when speaking of mixed blessings, my good fortune has caused problems in my family. My brothers and sisters and their children think I'm a terrible cheapskate because I haven't given them anything. They feel they are entitled to something, even though we have never been that close. I may one day give them something, but right now I don't feel like it. They pester me so. It's annoying. They call me names over the telephone. But as I said, we've never been close. And I never liked the way Sylvie and Lucille treated my sister, Celeste, who now lives with me. Celeste is handicapped. She never really developed as an adult. Something was wrong from the beginning. I think she was premature, but there was something else about the birth. My mother never liked to talk about it. Anyway, Celeste still has the mind of a child of six or seven years. But I've always loved her. She is three years older than me, eighty now, and we get along together. We always have."

She had finished her glass of wine and now wagged the empty glass at him. "Blessed Mary, this just may be the best wine I have ever tasted. I should come here more often."

"You should," he said, "and with me." Refilling their glasses, he said, "You know, these past weeks I've been thinking of little except my time with you and Gabriel during that summer so long ago. After my daughter's death last October, I thought I wanted to die too. I couldn't take my mind off this enormous hole in my life. For weeks I seldom left my apartment, going out only to buy food or stop at the liquor store for whisky. Most nights I scarcely slept more than two or three hours. Nothing in my life seemed worthwhile anymore. I shunned friends, and my poor daughter-in-law was beside herself trying to help me. My son is now divorced and lives in California with another woman. I couldn't even find a book that would take me out of myself. Books that have been faithful companions since I was a boy were useless, and during those months I could not settle down with one of them. My daughter-in-law would bring over armfuls of books from the self-help section of the library. Books written by psychologists and people called grief counsellors urging me to embrace this or that. I found them unreadable and trivial. What did they know of my sadness? Then a few months ago, to take my mind off Susan, I began to think, at night in bed, of that summer in Gaspé with you and Gabriel. I tried to remember details of how you looked as you walked along the shore of that long beach. And I would finally get to sleep soothed by the notion that I had experienced genuine happiness down there, even if I didn't appear to be all that happy at the time. And thinking about that at one o'clock in the morning helped me towards sleep. Yes, I was a sorehead, but I was also in love for the first time in my life. All of that feeling stayed with me during those nights and helped me realize how wonderful that summer truly was."

She was smiling, but he could see tears in her eyes. "Ah, James," she said, reaching across the table again for his hand, "I'm glad at least that remembering me like that has meant so much to you." She finished her wine, then put the glass down and laughed. "And here we are. Two old survivors getting drunk." She leaned across the table and spoke softly. "Let's enjoy ourselves tonight."

"Yes," he said. "As you say, we are survivors." He refilled their glasses.

"Let's drink to that," she said, and they raised their glasses. "To survival. And thank God for wine."

"To wine," they both said together, and as if on cue the waiter appeared with their meals. So, he thought, she was an elderly drinker like himself. He'd read a magazine article recently on how old people were now living longer than at any time in human history and often taking to the bottle to ease the burdens and worries of extended life. But if it gave you two or three hours of happiness, so what?

"You know, Odette," he said, "I was heartbroken that it was Gabriel and not me that you liked."

"I liked you well enough," she said. "I just liked Gabriel in another way."

"Perhaps you felt sorry for him. Crippled by polio and in that wheelchair since he was a child."

"Yes, perhaps, but I also liked him for his attitude. His spirit, if you like. Gabriel wasn't going to let that polio get the better of him, and I liked him for that. It took courage to face the life ahead of him. And I admired that."

"And you were right to do so," he said. "I suppose I was too young and selfish and too much taken with you to see all that."

"Well, you saw yourself as a rival maybe, and I can't imagine a fourteen-year-old boy has anything good to say about a rival. But Gabriel really liked you, James. He always spoke of you and was often hurt when you didn't spend more time with him. But never mind. Those days are gone and finished and here we are. This veal is delicious, by the way. How is your chicken?"

"Everything is good, Odette."

"Tell me now, what have you done with your life?"

"My life has not been terribly exciting, Odette. My students liked me, I think. I didn't play favourites. I was married to a lovely woman. An excellent wife and mother. Unfortunately she died in her fifties from breast cancer. A long time ago now. Nineteen eighty. Twenty-six years ago. We had two children, a boy and a girl. I spent my life teaching English at the University of Toronto. Had my share of sabbaticals. We lived in England one year while I worked on a book about the poet Tennyson, but I never finished it and perhaps it's just as well. I didn't think then and still don't that the world needs another book on Tennyson. But life itself was pretty good until Leah got sick." He paused, looking for the right words. "But my wife's death: of course I loved her, but her death . . . well, in time I got over it and carried on. It wasn't really like what happened two years ago when my daughter phoned from England to say that she had cancer. She must have been carrying the gene. To say that I was utterly devastated by the news would be an understatement. Then there was a terrible year of treatment and waiting. Always waiting for the inevitable and the asking of endless questions. Utterly pointless, but still you ask them at three o'clock in the morning. Anyway, there was all that until last October and then she was gone."

Odette had been listening carefully. "James, I'm so sorry."

"Yes. Well. The cruelty was also in the timing of it all. Susan's diagnosis came just months after she had been appointed principal of an outstanding girls' school in England. Everything seemed to be working out for her and then, like some kind of bad celestial joke, a death sentence. As soon as I heard Susan's terrible news that autumn of 2004, I flew to England to spend some time with her at Woolford Abbey. She was still able to carry on her duties. After our visit, I spent a couple of days in London, walking about the city and remembering the year I spent there with my family working on poor old Tennyson. I walked a great deal in those two days, asking myself the inevitable foolish questions and remembering happier days in a city I've always loved.

"And then a day or two before I was scheduled to come home, by sheer coincidence, whom should I meet in London but our old friend, Gabriel Fontaine. I was passing the Dorchester, a fancy hotel in Mayfair, when I saw a frail old man being helped out of a big American car by a young man. Of course, I didn't immediately recognize him, but then he said something and I thought I recognized the voice. Or maybe it was more the expression he used, an expression from the past, the nineteen thirties or forties. I suppose in carrying him from the car to the wheelchair, the young man hurt him a little, because I heard this frail old man call out, 'Easy, Adam, for crying out loud.' It wasn't an expression you hear much but it sounded like something Gabriel would say. It wasn't like me to do something like this, but I hurried over and introduced myself, trying not to sound like some crazed street person asking for money. At first of course he looked up from his chair with a rather surly face.

I imagined his brain was trying to figure out who this stranger was. I asked him if he remembered me from the summer of 1944 when he and his mother had stayed at the St. Lawrence Hotel in Percé, Quebec. And then suddenly he smiled. A wonderful smile. 'Yes,' he said, 'and you were there. You used to push my chair around that village. We'd go down to the wharf and watch the fishermen and the tourist boats taking people to that island where they had all those birds. Millions of birds crapping over everything. I remember that. We went on a boat ride around that island once. And your name is Hiller or Miller.'

" 'Hillyer,' I said, 'James Hillyer.'

"It was all connecting in his mind and he was so happy to see me; in fact, he invited me to have dinner with him that evening in the hotel. And we did. We talked about that summer in 1944. He remembered most of it but got some things wrong, including his recollection of me as a friend. By the end of that summer I was disgusted by the way he treated you."

Odette smiled a little sadly. "And did he remember me, James?"

"Of course." He didn't tell her that Gabriel had forgotten her name. At dinner that evening Gabriel had remembered her as Yvette, asking James, "Remember that French girl, Yvette?" They had had a little disagreement about her correct name, but he wasn't going to tell her that. Nobody likes to be told that someone we were once close to has forgotten our name.

"I could tell from the look of him that he was a very sick man, and that evening at dinner he told me he had pancreatic cancer and was on his way to an assisted suicide clinic in Switzerland. He and the young man Adam were leaving in two days and he asked me if I would go along."

"He asked you to go with him and watch him die?"

"Yes. I know it sounds rather grisly, but he pleaded with me that evening. I still don't know why I agreed, but I really had no plans for the next two days, and I suppose I felt sorry for him. Besides, I was more or less at my wits' end with worry about Susan. Maybe I even wondered if this way to die might be an option for her. I honestly can't remember, but in any case I went. Gabriel paid for everything, of course: first class on Swiss International and an expensive hotel in Zurich. Gabriel was a very rich man. He'd made his money in the stock market. He told me that he'd married three times and all his marriages had ended in divorce. He had no children. And I sensed that he had no close friends. It must have seemed to him that I was the best he could hope for at the end of his life. So I went to that clinic and watched him die. It didn't take long."

"Poor Gabriel."

"Well, yes, you could say that, but I would guess there are many terminally ill people who would envy Gabriel's death. No choking, no struggling for breath, no sucking on ice cubes. He was given a sedative and then took a pill and went to sleep. An untroubled descent into oblivion, I thought at the time, and still do."

Her glass was empty again and so was his. "It's quite a story, James. It was good of you to go with Gabriel to that place."

"How about a glass of brandy or Calvados to finish our meal?"

"An excellent idea," she said. "I have become very fond of Courvoisier." Her eyes were glistening again. "You were very kind to me at the end of that summer, James. When I told you I was pregnant, you gave me some money. Remember? I think it was the night before you left to go home on the train."

"Yes, I do remember. It wasn't much."

"It was twenty-five dollars. A fortune to me at the time."

"Did you have a child then? You were so young."

"Yes, I was only fifteen. I wouldn't be sixteen until December. My father had found a place for us on rue Blanchard. A cold-water flat. A terrible place really, but a roof over our heads. That's about all you could say for it. I couldn't bear the thought of telling my mother and father that I was pregnant, so I looked up a girl I'd heard of. I had thought about this from the minute I knew I was pregnant. Thought about it all the way to Montreal sitting beside my father in the cab of somebody's truck. My brothers and sisters were in the back of the truck. All the way to Montreal. My mother and Celeste had gone by train. This girl used to live near us and she had an aunt who was known to perform the operation."

"You're talking about an abortion, right?"

"Yes. And this girl told me it would cost fifty dollars. I can't remember how I got the rest of the money. It was a long time ago. I have a vague memory of cleaning flats for some landlord. However I did get it, and I went to this woman's place."

"You were only fifteen. You must have been terrified."

"Terrified?" She shrugged. "I don't know. I suppose I was frightened, but I didn't know what to expect. I think I just wanted to get it over with. The woman took the money and then she gave me something to drink. I think it was whisky and water. I choked it down, and then she gave me a piece of rubber tubing to bite on."

"My God, Odette."

"Yes, James, that's how it was done in St. Henri in 1944. It was awful. She hurt me, that woman. I can just remember lying on this mattress and the woman was kneeling between my legs. I could see past her grey head. The door to the kitchen was open and this girl, the aunt's niece, was sitting at the kitchen table reading a comic book and eating these Cracker Jacks. Do you remember those things? So sticky and sweet."

"Yes, I do."

Odette leaned forward and whispered, "Jesus Christ, she was ten feet away eating Cracker Jacks while I was biting on a piece of rubber tubing to keep from yelling. What a pathetic story, eh, James?"

"You did what you thought you had to do at the time. You were so young. But you took an awful risk. You could have died."

"Yes, and at the time I might not have cared. For weeks I kept wondering if I shouldn't have gone to the convent over on rue St. Agnès, where they took in unwed mothers. But I have never liked nuns. At school they always seemed so humourless and cruel. They'd hit you on the knuckles with their rulers over the silliest things.

"So there it was. I had done it and I walked home that night with an old towel between my legs. It wasn't far. A couple of blocks. Crept into that apartment and went to bed. I shared a bed with Sylvie but I didn't say anything to her. We never got along. Maybe she was asleep. I don't remember. But the next day I told her I was sick and couldn't go to school. And after my mother had fed everybody and they'd all left, she came in to see me. Felt my head and then pulled back the covers and saw the blood-soaked towel. Dear God, I can still remember the look of horror on her face. She made the sign of the cross and then began to cry. 'You've had one of those operations, haven't you?' she asked. I was crying by then too, mostly from seeing the disappointment and misery on her face. But you know what? She looked after me, my mother. I think she was too ashamed to go to a doctor, so she took it upon herself. At first she told the others I had the flu, but I'm sure they knew, and Sylvie never let me forget it. Even up to now. Just a few weeks ago Sylvie asked me for some money and I said I didn't feel like giving her any and she said, 'You always were a little whore, Odette. Even as a kid when you got knocked up by your fancy American boyfriend.' Nice, eh? After over sixty years that's what she still thinks of me. And she used to say that it was me who drove our father away. She knew how to hurt me because maybe she was right. My poor father. I think I was his favourite, and when he found out what I'd done, he could hardly believe it. And the abortion may have finished him. He had lost his job and couldn't find another one that would pay as well as the munitions factory. Do you remember my father, James? He came down to Gaspé at the end of that summer to take us back to Montreal. I think you met him."

"Yes, I do remember your father."

"He was a very intelligent man and spent a year in a seminary. But he told me once that he read too many books and decided that he no longer wanted to be a priest and so he gave it up. Unfortunately he didn't go to university or pursue any particular career, and then he got married because my mother was pregnant with Celeste, and after that he just had to work at whatever he could get. As long as the war was on, he did well enough in the munitions factory, but then he got laid off and he couldn't find anything else that paid as well. And he had a lot of mouths to feed. By the time he came down to Gaspé at the end of the summer, he was feeling down, though only I seemed to notice it and I said nothing to the others. But when he got back to Montreal, he wasn't interested in anything. He began to spend his afternoons in the taverns with his books. He seemed to have no friends. So maybe what I did that year when I was only fifteen finished him. One day that fall he just left us. Told my mother one morning he was going to see about a job in some factory. We never saw him again, and some thought he might have drowned himself in the St. Lawrence River. But over the years we also heard rumours about him being somewhere in the States, in Vermont or Massachusetts. Married with children. We don't really know. All I know is that he left us after he found out about me, and I have carried the guilt all my life, because I loved my father very much."

The waiter brought their drinks, and after he left, Odette said, "I think I'm a little drunk, James, so enough of these sad old memories. After these drinks, can we get the bill and then perhaps go for a walk? I'd like to clear my head. I think it's still daylight out there. Maybe we could go to the Terrace and look at the river."

"A good idea," he said. "Let's do that."

When the waiter brought the bill, she picked it up at once and put on her glasses. "Why don't I just take care of all this? I've enjoyed myself so much this evening. You're a very good listener, and I've never had too many people in my life who were good listeners. But then I talk too much. Always have."

"You've had quite a life, Odette, and I've enjoyed listening to you. But I don't want you to pay for the meal. Let's just split the bill."

She laughed. "Still the stubborn boy I remember, eh. All right."

When they left the hotel, the evening sky was still radiant

with light and she slipped her hand into his as they walked to Dufferin Terrace among others who were ambling by or leaning on the railing to look down at the river. He liked the feel of her warm hand in his, and he felt quite suddenly like kissing her cheek and he did. She looked up at him and smiled and for a few minutes they stood by the railing. Then they walked across to the little park and sat on the bench where that afternoon he had watched a young father playing hide-and-seek with his son while his wife sat on a bench with the baby. What happiness he had found in looking at the young family. And now another kind of happiness with Odette, though in profile she looked grave in the waning light from between the upper branches of the trees. But they were still holding hands as they sat there and Odette said, "I have something else to tell you about myself. Something you need to know. I don't suppose you smoke, do you?"

"No, I don't, Odette. Why?"

"Oh, I just suddenly felt like having a cigarette. Which is crazy because I haven't smoked for years now. Five or six, at least. But never mind." She looked across the park at the lights of the big hotel and the darkened figures of people walking on the Terrace. "Lately, I've been having trouble with a man who has been a part of my life for a long time. I hadn't seen him for three or four years. He was in Bordeaux Prison for some of that time. Anyway, the next thing I find out is that he's moved in with his sister and brother-in-law who live in Sainte Foy." She had turned to him. "Do you know where that is?"

"No, I'm afraid not."

"It's a suburb of this city. He's a half-hour bus ride from my front door."

"So this man is bothering you now?"

"Yes, he's bothering me now. His sister told him about the lottery win, and now Raoul would not only like some money, he'd also like to move in with Celeste and me. Raoul is now what? Five years older than me, so eighty-two. And he's making a nuisance of himself. And because of his age he also has this disease. At least, that's what Monique says. He has this disease that old people sometimes get when they lose their memory and become confused."

"Alzheimer's."

"Yes, Alzheimer's. It's just beginning, Monique said, and sometimes he's all right, but then at other times he's a handful. He came to the house once and it was difficult. Do you remember that Sunday night I phoned you and told you not to come here that week?"

"I do, yes, and I knew something was up. You sounded edgy."

"Well, I was. That was the day Raoul turned up. Monique and Bertrand, her husband, brought him. The whole afternoon was very upsetting. He didn't want to leave and was making a fuss. I gave him some money that day and he finally left. I think I made a mistake in giving him the money. He'll probably be after me for more."

He said, "It's none of my business, I suppose, but since you brought this man's name up, I have to ask why would you have him in your house in the first place?"

"It's a good question and to tell you the truth, I don't know." She was staring at the darkening trees. "I suppose I felt sorry for him in a way. He has this Alzheimer's disease and he has no money or very little, just his old-age pension, I imagine. But he's now convinced himself that we are married, though we're not and never have been; according to his sister that was all he talked about. After Monique told him about my lottery win, he asked her every day to tell him where his wife lived. Now he feels entitled to be looked after by me and live in my house, which of course he sees as half his. Goddamn it, I shouldn't have given him money that Sunday. That was a serious mistake. He'll be expecting it all the time now. But I just wanted him out of my house. My God, the man appeared at my door holding this pitiful little bouquet of flowers. He probably picked them from a public garden. He looked like a big kid on a date standing there on the other side of my front door. Then later when I told him that living in my house was impossible, he began to cry. Pulled out all the stops and bawled there in my kitchen with his arms on the table and his head down. Going on about how big the house was and there was room for him. 'Four bedrooms,' he kept saying. 'You have four bedrooms, Odette. Why couldn't I have one of those?' Honest to God, I thought I'd go out of my mind listening to him. And then Celeste started to cry. You see, my sister likes Raoul. She sees him as a big brother or something, I don't know. But they get along. Watch cartoons together, for Christ's sake. But he is good with her. She's no threat, see. A simple-minded eighty-year-old woman and he has always liked her. Now I had to listen to her too. 'Why can't Raoul stay, Odette?' she kept saying. I don't think she ever believed me when I would tell her how he treated me when I lived with him years ago. And anyway, even if she did at the time, she's long forgotten it."

He watched her shake her head in dismay and he put his arm around her. He could tell that she was close to tears. "I came to this city to get away from the others, and my past follows me here. You see what a mess I'm in. A few weeks ago Monique and Bertrand put him into a home, La Résidence, in Sainte Foy. He was just too much for them and I think his presence in the house made Bertrand nervous. He's a small, mild-mannered fellow, a retired civil servant, and maybe his brother-in-law intimidated him—is that the word in English?"

"Yes, intimidated. Frightened."

"Exactly. Do you remember how you used to help me with English words and phrases that summer?"

"Yes, I do."

"Good," and she abruptly kissed him on the lips. "So they put Raoul in this place in Sainte Foy, but I gather he isn't happy there, and how long they can keep him in La Résidence, I don't know. At first he was sharing a room with another man who also has Alzheimer's, but that didn't last more than a week, according to Monique. Raoul and this man had a quarrel over something silly, a game show on television, I think, and one day Raoul pulled all the man's clothing off their hangers in the closet and threw everything on the floor. Then he threatened him. Apparently shook his fist at him and so on. He's a big man, Raoul, and you don't want him to get his hands on you. Believe me, I know what it's like. So, of course, the poor man complained and the director of La Résidence—who by the way is a woman and Raoul wouldn't like that, a woman telling him what to do—told Monique and Bertrand that Raoul would have to live in a private room that would cost more money. I told them I would help pay for that. And yes, I know I'm inconsistent but I wanted to help in some way. I mean, damn it all, I don't want to see the man on the street. I want him looked after in a proper place as long as he stays out of my home and life.

"But it seems that he has taken to wandering. Some people with that disease wander away and get lost. It's a big worry for the people in that place, and my understanding is that the director has warned Raoul and his sister that if he keeps leaving by himself without permission, he might have to find another place to live. Raoul Cloutier is a dangerous man, James. When he was younger, he crippled a man in a bar fight. Nearly killed him. They put him in Donnacona Prison for that. He was sentenced to five years, though I think he only served three and a half or four. It was a long time ago."

"You shouldn't have to live in fear of this man, Odette. Have you been in touch with the police at all? But when I think of it, I suppose he would have to break the law before the police get involved."

"Yes," she said, "and breaking the law might mean breaking parts of me."

"We'll work something out."

She smiled and took his hand. "Well, just being with someone who will listen is a good start. I don't want you to get involved with any of this, but I want you to know that I'm very glad that you came to Quebec to see me after all those years."

"Maybe we should go for a nightcap," he said.

"Yes, let's do that. A nightcap to send us off to sleep."

They got up from the bench holding hands and set off across the park towards rue St. Louis. "Where did you meet this Raoul Cloutier?"

She squeezed his hand. "Let's get a drink first and then I'll tell you a bedtime story about this old lady's younger days." She laughed. As they passed through Porte St. Louis to the Grande Allée, he was thinking that in many ways Odette was still the mischievous girl he remembered from that summer in Gaspé.

The Grande Allée was crowded and the bars busy. They could hear laughter and music coming from some of them. This was life too, he thought. And it had been going on during all those empty nights he endured in his apartment. What was life worth if you did nothing with it? If you sat alone in an apartment drinking to forget the past? On this warm summer evening, he vowed he would pay more attention to simple pleasures. Like walking with someone whose company you enjoyed. Even in old age there were moments to savour, pleasures to anticipate and enjoy.

They sat at an outside table so they could watch the mostly young crowd passing by on the street. He ordered two glasses of Courvoisier from the young waitress, who seemed amused in a pleasant way by their appearance among the young, and he felt proud to be there with Odette, enjoying the friendly commotion of this beautiful city at night. Odette took a sip of the brandy and said, "I met Raoul Cloutier when I was quite young. I was nineteen. Not so long after that summer when we were kids, but I had learned a great deal about life in those four years. I had lied about my age and was working at a bar on Ste. Catherine Street in Montreal. Mostly an Anglo place, but my English was pretty good then. Remember how you used to correct me when I used a certain expression and didn't get it right?"

He shrugged. "Yes. Mr. Know-it-all at fourteen."

"No, no, James." She smiled. "Well, yes, you were a know-it-all but I didn't mind because I needed somebody to help me. Anyway, one evening I was serving this older man, maybe in his fifties, a nice guy, very polite, and he asked me how much money I earned with tips and everything in a week. I could have

told him to get lost, that it was none of his business, but he was
such a nice guy that I didn't take offence. I didn't tell him how
much I made either because it really wasn't very much, but it
didn't matter because he said, 'Whatever it is, I'll double it if
you come and work for me.' Okay, the first thing that came to
mind was prostitution. I was thinking he runs a cathouse and
is looking for young whores. So I just laughed at him and said,
'I may not make much money, mister, but that doesn't mean
I'm for sale.' But he just went on in his nice manner and quiet
way. It was as if he was reading my mind, because then he said,
'It's not what you think. I have a legitimate entertainment business near Rivière du Loup. I now have five girls working for me
and I need another. The girls work as professional entertainers.
It's all above board, believe me. You are a very attractive young
woman and I think you would be very good in this line of work.
I can guarantee at least double what you are earning here and
you can share a room with two other girls above the bar at no
charge. The police inspect the place every night. There's nothing illegal about it. It's just entertainment. I've had girls work
for me for a few years who have saved enough money to buy
a house. One girl still sends me a Christmas card. She paid for
her university education and is now a chartered accountant and
works for one of the largest corporations in the province.' And
so to make a long story short, I went to work for Mr. Alphonse
at his roadhouse, the Green Mermaid on Highway 132 a few
miles from Rivière du Loup. I was a stripper, James. A couple
of the girls taught me the moves in an afternoon. It wasn't hard.
So while I'm not particularly proud of having taken off most
of my clothes in front of a roomful of horny men, neither am I
particularly ashamed. It was a job that paid well and I saved a lot

of money. And unlike one or two of the other girls, I didn't fuck the customers after work. And that's where I met Raoul Cloutier. He was one of the three bouncers at the Green Mermaid, a big, good-looking guy who made it quite clear early on that he was interested. And of course he watched out for me, made sure that nobody bothered me after the show. I guess I fell in love with him. In those days I liked being with Raoul because people gave him plenty of room. He always made sure that none of the creepy ones got too close. All the other girls were jealous of me, but I didn't care.

"I had been living for a while in that apartment on the second floor of the roadhouse, but Raoul and I decided to move in together and we got a nice little flat in Rivière du Loup. Life then was pretty good. We were young and we had money. Early on, though, I could see that Raoul had a bad temper. He was easily frustrated and then he could be difficult. Most of the time I could joke him out of his moods, but a few times he slapped my face or pushed me out of the way if he was going to another room to sulk. He could be rough too with customers at the roadhouse and Mr. Alphonse kept warning him. I remember him saying once, 'Just escort the guy out the door, Raoul. You don't have to lay a hand on him. Take him outside and tell him he's welcome back when he's sober.' But that wasn't Raoul's style. There are always guys who drink too much and are looking for trouble, and so there were fights and Raoul took care of that easily. But he treated everybody the same, so if some guy was just mouthing off after a few beers, Raoul would manhandle him out the door. He simply didn't know how to be reasonable, and eventually Mr. Alphonse fired him.

"I'd been working there for nearly two years and Mr.

Alphonse liked me, but he had to move his girls from time to time because the customers liked a change of scenery. So when I said I was leaving, he didn't argue. In fact, he told me he thought I would be better off in a different job. Raoul and I then decided to get married. We would move to Montreal and we'd find work and then get married. He wanted to be a professional wrestler like his hero Yvon Robert, who was then the most popular wrestler in Quebec. A big handsome guy who made a lot of money, and Raoul wanted to be just like him. He was going to take lessons at some gym.

"We found an apartment on rue Ambroise in St. Henri, not all that far from where I grew up. Rent was still pretty cheap then in St. Henri. At night Raoul and I would lie awake and he would talk about being a wrestler and making a lot of money and then buying a farm just like the one where he grew up. And we'd have lots of kids. He wanted ten or eleven children, mostly boys to carry on the family name. But who said I wanted to be a farmer's wife with a brood of kids? And how could I tell him that if we married, there would be no children in our lives? A few weeks after we started living together in Rivière du Loup, I'd gone to a doctor because I was having pain in my uterus. He sent me to a gynecologist, who examined me and said, 'You've had an abortion, haven't you?' 'Yes,' I said, and he told me he was sorry but whoever did it was clumsy, and he didn't think I could now have children. A lot of my stuff down there had been damaged. He gave me some pills for the pain and said it would clear up. But as for 'children in my future'—I remember that phrase—it was out of the question. So lying there listening to Raoul's pipe dream, I kept wondering how I was going to tell him all this. I could just imagine his disappointment and anger. And then, of course, there would be slaps. A lifetime of slaps across the face whenever I disagreed with him, and he would be sorry for hitting me and start bawling and telling me how much he loved me and he wouldn't do it again. And of course, I must have thought that he would change or that I could change him or something equally foolish, because I agreed to marry this man.

"So a few nights before the wedding we had a rehearsal at this church in St. Henri. One of the girls from the Green Mermaid was my . . . what's it? Maid of honour. And it went all right and everybody was happy. And now I think that in his old age and with this disease, Raoul has confused that rehearsal of the wedding with the real thing, which never happened. That's my guess anyway. On that night of the rehearsal we went out afterwards and had a few drinks and when we got back to the apartment, I decided to tell him the truth about my inability to have children. I knew he would take it hard, but I was hoping for a little understanding. I told him I wanted to be honest and fair with him. Tell him the truth about it all, my pregnancy at fifteen, the awful experience with that woman and her niece reading comic books and eating Cracker Jacks while her aunt ruined my insides. So I did and he just kept looking at me with this frown. And then after I finished, he got up from his chair and came over and gave me this slap across the face, calling me a whore from hell. I remember that particular priceless phrase, a *whore from hell*. Then he began to slap me around with those big hands. I fought back, pulled his hair, and even punched him once right on the nose. I was crying and swearing and we were yelling at one another. The whole building must have heard us, and somebody called the police because I could hear a siren. I kept telling him to let me go, but he had this grip on my wrist and I felt this terrible pain going up my arm and I blacked out. When I came around, Raoul was holding me and crying and the police were at the door. It didn't take long to see that my wrist was broken, and the police asked if I wanted to lay charges and I said no, because in those few minutes of our fight, I'd already decided that marrying Raoul Cloutier would be the mistake of my lifetime.

"That night he took me to the hospital and I had my wrist put in a cast. When we got home, he wanted to have sex. I just wanted to sleep, but I'd learned long ago that you gave him what he wanted or you paid for it. So he got on me for his usual minute and a half, and afterwards he was all lovey-dovey, asking me how I liked it as he always did. Christ, I was so mad I could have spit in his face. So I said, 'You know, Raoul. I would settle for half of that thing of yours on a nicer man.' He didn't say anything to that but I could tell he was angry and he probably wanted to give me another cuff. But he just turned on his side and lay there and soon he was snoring. The next morning he had to take his car into the garage, and while he was gone, I packed my clothes and called a taxi. I moved in with my sister Sylvie until I got my own place.

"I put up with her snide comments about my choice of men and I looked for work. I spent some more time as a waitress, and then I worked at the airport for a few years as a clerk. We wore uniforms and funny little hats in those days as we checked people onto their flights and attached stickers to their baggage. Air Canada was then called Trans-Canada Air Lines, but I can't remember now what the Montreal airport was called before they named it after Pierre Trudeau. Anyway, there I met a nice guy named Marcel Dubé. He was going on a trip and I checked him through while he kidded around about how pretty I was, and then just before he left he asked if I would go out with him some night. I guess you could call it a hunch, but I gave him my phone number and a couple of weeks later he called me and we went out. We had dinner and saw a movie, and I can still remember that movie. It was called *On the Waterfront* with Marlon Brando, and the funny thing was that Marcel kind of looked like Brando. He was in his late thirties then and stocky, well built like Brando. His hair was thinning a bit, but he was still a very good-looking man, and I told him he looked like a movie star. He just laughed. He had no conceit in him at all, Marcel. We really hit it off, and he asked me if I would like to work for him. He owned a fleet of taxis, about ten or twelve at the time, although ten years later he had twice as many. He said he needed another dispatcher and thought I could do the job. You know, you answer the phone and then send the cabs here and there all over the city. I liked it, and I worked for Marcel for thirty years, believe it or not.

"I moved out of Sylvie's and got my own place on rue Antoine, and in case you're wondering, James, yes, Marcel and I had a relationship. And yes, he had a wife and children, but he wasn't happy in the marriage. We had a good thing going for two or three years, but the passion and novelty gradually faded and we became just friends. That's unusual, don't you think? You have an affair with someone and then you both decide that it's all over, but that is no reason why you can't still remain friends. That's how it was with Marcel and me. As I said, I continued to work for him all those years. Sometimes we'd go out for a drink after work. But no more sex. Just friendship. A very good man, Marcel Dubé, and over the years I would miss him. He died from cancer in his fifties."

"But you must have seen more of Raoul Cloutier over those years, Odette."

"Oh yes. Fool that I was, I lived with him off and on. As he got older, he didn't seem to be as rough as he was in earlier days, though of course he was still Raoul, moody, impatient, and suspicious. So we'd share a flat until we got tired of one another, or he'd be convicted of some theft or assault and go to Bordeaux for a few months. But he had a way of showing up at my door after he was released from prison or had been kicked out by some girlfriend. My God, James, listening to all this, all the men in my life, you must think what a tramp I was, but really I never saw myself that way. I wasn't very well educated. I had to learn many things as I went along, and I didn't always make the right decisions. But I don't spend a lot of time worrying about that. I am what I am and was." She finished her brandy. "Anyway, I wanted to be honest with you about my past." She was looking out at the street and the people. "Look at us now," she said with a laugh. "We must be the oldest on the street."

"It's funny," he said, "but I've been thinking the same thing. But so what?" he added. "I'm just happy to be with you."

"Well, good then," she said. "And the same goes for me with you here, James." And again she reached across the table with both hands and touched his. Then they both watched a young couple climbing into a calèche. The young man was very attentive, and when they were settled, he kissed the girl as the driver touched the old horse lightly with his crop and the carriage moved off, the hoofs sounding on the pavement. Odette watched them leave. "All that sex ahead of them," she said, smiling. "Now that you are an old fellow, James, do you miss it?" For a moment he was distracted by the very fact that he was sitting at a table on this busy street in Quebec City at ten o'clock on a summer night. "Sorry, Odette. Miss what?"

"Sex. You know, the old commotion with its shrieks and howls and yes, yes, yes?"

He laughed. "Shrieks and howls? I don't remember too much of that, but yes, I suppose I do at times. I can't pretend it bothers me every day."

"No, of course not. At our age. But now and then an old itch, eh?"

"Yes. An old itch is a good way to put it."

"And not easily scratched when you're in your seventies."

"Not easily, no."

"But an itch just the same."

"Without a doubt." They were both laughing now. "When was the last time you had sex, James?"

How wonderfully direct Odette was! He had liked that about her from the first day all those years ago. She was the most completely unselfconscious person he had ever known. "To tell you the truth, I can't remember." But in fact he could dimly recall it even though it was hardly memorable, an awkward fumbling between two people who found themselves alone together and seemed as clumsy and shy with each other as two virgins. He and Anne Sinclair had known one another for years. Anne, a tall, blond, icily Nordic woman who taught French at the university, was friendly enough to talk to but with a natural reserve that seemed to discourage any attempt at intimacy. Or at least that had been his impression of Anne. He had always guessed that she was perhaps a closet lesbian. But one night after a faculty party they found themselves together on the steps of Hart House waiting for a taxi. On a whim he asked her home for a nightcap; he had been a widower for ten years and she was tall and shy, in her late thirties or maybe forty by then. And once in his apartment after their drink, it seemed inevitable that they should embrace and kiss, though both seemed hesitant. But finally in the bedroom they managed to undress one another and climb into bed. She told him that she had experienced sex only once before when she was a university student and that unhappy event seemed to colour their performance. They were both nonplussed at finding themselves naked together in bed: a kind of Victorian scene, he imagined, with poor Anne not quite sure of how to let herself go and enjoy what most people take as a natural pleasure. Perhaps he was to blame. Her diffidence seemed to encumber him, but they managed a somewhat clumsy copulation that wasn't in the least memorable for either of them. Certainly it was never referred to as they carried on their casual acquaintanceship as colleagues, and not once over the years that followed did they mention that evening. And that would have been fifteen or twenty years ago, he guessed. Odette was looking at him with what he could only describe as a wry grin. "So long ago you can't even remember, eh, James?"

"I'm afraid so, Odette. At least ten or fifteen years."

Odette shook her head. "That's a long time between fucks for sure, though I suppose that's what happens to us if we live long enough. A girlfriend once told me to buy a vibrator. She said it did the job and the best thing was you didn't have to make his breakfast next morning. Or listen to some blah, blah, blah about how his wife didn't understand him. So I bought one and it was okay. It did the job, I suppose, but I didn't like the idea of being fucked by a machine. I missed the human touch."

A couple had just sat down at the next table and must have overheard Odette's observation because they looked at one another with wonderful grins. Odette, of course, had taken no notice of them but only said, "Do you know what I'd like to do tomorrow, James?"

"What would you like to do tomorrow, Odette?"

"I'd like to show you Île d'Orléans. It's a wonderful place to visit. Very peaceful. I'm told the Indians called it the Island of Enchantment. We could take a tour bus. I'd like to bring along Celeste too. You'll like her, James. She can't speak English very well, only understands a bit, but she's gentle and kind. And like a little kid, she's easily pleased if you show her some kindness and I know you will. Maybe we could go to the big church at Beaupré. Ste. Anne de Beaupré. Churches don't do anything for me, but Celeste is very devout, and when I took her to the Basilica at Beaupré in the spring, she just loved it. All those crutches and canes on the front wall are the first things you see when you walk into the big church. All the crippled people who once used them were cured and left them behind. A place of miracles, eh! Celeste just loved it. A holy place, she called it. Celeste goes to Mass every Sunday. When we lived in Montreal, I used to take her to the big church in St. Henri Square. I never took communion myself. That's all behind me. I've outgrown it all. To me it's just—there's an expression in English I like, James, to describe something that isn't what it seems—smoke and mirrors, is that it?"

"Yes. Smoke and mirrors. A kind of delusion."

"Exactly. But I have always encouraged Celeste to carry on with her religion. To say her prayers every night before sleep and count her beads. I wouldn't dream of coming between her and her beliefs. She used to ask me why I didn't pray like her, but over the years she has come to accept the fact that I'm no longer interested. Sometimes she worries about how I will get to Heaven to be with her when she dies. Given the way I've lived my life, I can't imagine anything more unlikely than there being a Heaven with me in it. But I don't say that. I just shrug and tell her not to worry about me.

"When we moved here I used to take her to a church not too far away from our house, but then a neighbour who lives just down the street noticed us at church and took a liking to Celeste, so now she takes her. Off they go each Sunday while I stay home and read the weekend paper. Anyway, tomorrow let's take her to her favourite church in Beaupré. We may have to find another bus. Beaupré is not on the island. It's on the north shore of the river. But it's not that far."

"Why don't I rent a car for the day?" he said. "It will give us more flexibility. We can come and go as we like and not be bothered with all the sightseers."

"You can drive, then?"

"Of course. Who can't nowadays?"

"Well, me for one. Living most of my life in Montreal, I never saw the need, and now that I can afford any car you could name, I wouldn't have any idea of how to drive one. But really I don't want the responsibility. I'm too old now to learn. But listen, if you drive us tomorrow, I'll make a lunch and we'll have a picnic. We'll look around the island in the morning and after lunch we'll take Celeste to her favourite church. Agreed, old man?"

"Agreed," he said.

"Now I'm tired," she said. "All that wine and brandy we drank. What a pair of old sots we are, James. But never mind, we are still alive, eh? Let's find a taxi for me."

Odette

They had parted with a final kiss and he had helped her into the taxi. It was a real kiss too and not just a peck on the cheek. A soulful kiss, she would say, a kiss she had enjoyed and would remember. As she walked up the steps to the front door, she could hear the music or the television and it seemed that every light in the house was burning. When she turned the key and opened the door, the blast of sound hit her. Throwing off her coat, she set about turning off the living and dining room lights, calling up the stairs to Celeste that she was home. All the light and noise was to be expected. Celeste could not go to bed when she was alone in a dark house. But now the television was turned off, and Odette went in to the kitchen, where on the counter she saw the opened jars of jam and peanut butter, a half-empty glass of milk. The kitchen clock said ten-thirty. A few minutes later Celeste appeared at the kitchen doorway, a tall, pale spectre in her nightgown and robe, her white hair falling to her shoulders; for a moment Odette thought she could have been looking at the ghost of her mother, dead now sixty years or more. "Celeste, you startled me."

"You're late, Odette."

"Yes and I am sorry, but listen, I have some wonderful news." Celeste was usually animated by good news but might not have heard, because she continued to stare at Odette. Of course, her hearing was no longer the best.

"I was worried," said Celeste. "I thought something had happened to you."

"Nothing happened to me. James and I were at a café on the Grande Allée. A beautiful summer evening and we talked and talked. Time got away from us. Now listen, tomorrow we are going to Île d'Orléans. James is going to rent a car so we won't have to bother with a bus. I'm going to make a picnic lunch for us in the morning. Afterwards we'll drive to Ste. Anne de Beaupré and visit the Basilica. You remember how much you enjoyed walking around the Basilica in the spring."

Celeste nodded and then smiled. Herself again. "Yes, the big church. It's very beautiful. A place for God's miracles. All those canes and crutches that crippled people threw away when they began to walk again."

"So tomorrow will be a busy day and we must get to bed."

Celeste said suddenly, "I forgot to tell you. Monique called about Raoul. He's in jail. The police picked him up for something. I can't remember what now. But she and Bertrand were going to get him out. It was a while ago when she phoned. Maybe seven or eight o'clock."

"Why was he at the police station? What did Raoul do?"

Again she felt those mixed feelings. Relief that he was no longer roaming the streets, but at the same time regret that he was in trouble again at his age.

Celeste said, "I think it had something to do with a phone booth."

"A phone booth?"

"Yes, he was doing something in a phone booth and a woman saw him and phoned the police."

Was he exposing himself? she wondered. "Christ," she said. "What next?"

"You shouldn't swear, Odette. God doesn't like swearing."

"I know, I know, I'm sorry. So Monique and Bertrand have gone to get him, that's good. I can't believe the police would lock him up. I'm sure they understand now that he doesn't know what he's doing half the time."

"I think they were going to get him and return him to the place where he's living."

"Yes. La Résidence. What's the matter with those people anyway? They should watch him more carefully."

She wondered about calling Monique, but it was late now, and anyway, she didn't want to become involved with Raoul's antics. She wanted to keep her distance from him. He was no longer a part of her life, or at least she liked to think that he wasn't. Yet Monique insisted on trying to keep her informed about every detail of Raoul's whereabouts. It was all so complicated, and already she felt the onset of a migraine. To distract herself, she went to the sink and began to wash Celeste's dishes. Her sister followed her across the kitchen and reached for a towel as she always did, though Odette wished she would go up to her room.

"Are you angry with me, Odette?" she asked.

"No, of course not. Why would I be angry with you?"

"I had all the lights in the house on. I guess I was using a lot of electricity, wasn't I?"

"Never mind the lights. It's okay. I don't care about the electricity."

"I like the light on at night when I am alone in the house."

"I know that. Don't worry about it."

"But remember how you used to tell me to turn off lights when I left a room? And here I was with all the lights on."

Odette sighed. "It's just an old habit with me, Celeste. When we were so hard up in St. Henri, it mattered. Don't you remember Maman scolding us if we didn't turn the lights off after we left a room? I must have picked it up from her. But it doesn't matter now and I'm not angry with you. James and I are going to take you to the big church tomorrow."

"Is James a Catholic, Odette?"

"I don't think so. I don't believe he is much interested in religion, but he's still a very good man. You will like him. Now let's clean all this up and get to bed. Tomorrow will be a big day for you. Okay?"

"Okay, Odette."

And so as always they climbed the stairs to their bedrooms across the hallway from one another. As she undressed, Odette could hear her sister's mumbled prayer. For as long as she could remember, she had tucked Celeste into bed. Now when she went into the room, her sister was still on her knees by the bedside, her hands pointed upward. Odette briefly knelt beside her and kissed her cheek. Odette waited until Celeste had finished and crossed herself. Then Odette helped her to her feet, said,

"Now to bed, Celeste," and pulled back the covers. "It's a little cool tonight. I've left the window open, the air is so fresh and clear, but I put an extra blanket on for you."

Celeste lay in bed looking up at her. Her glasses were still on. Odette gently lifted them off her face. "You don't want to go to sleep with those on, silly. If you roll over, you'll break them."

Celeste smiled up at her. "Thank you. And thank you for not being angry with me about the lights."

Odette tucked the blankets around her. "Nobody is angry with you. Now sleep and we will have a nice day together tomorrow."

"Do you want to sleep with me tonight, Odette?"

"Only if you need me in the night, but it's best, I think, for me to sleep alone. I have a little headache coming on."

"Can I get something for you?"

It was such a hopeless question. Get what for her and how? But her heart was in the right place, and Odette felt a wave of affection for her sister and kissed her forehead. "I'll be fine now; go to sleep and have good dreams. Just think of tomorrow and our trip to Ste. Anne's church. That will help you to sleep. Good night, Celeste."

"Good night and thank you for not being angry with me about the lights."

In her bedroom she swallowed two aspirin with her nightly glass of water and lay down, hoping for the best. She already knew that going to sleep would not be easy. Raoul was probably back at the home by now. But what next? She knew she would have to drink some more brandy to find sleep. It wasn't a good idea. Alcohol put you out but not for long, and she was beginning to rely on it too much. And yet the thought of lying there twitching through the night was unbearable. She waited for Celeste to fall asleep. If Celeste heard her walking about, she would be alarmed, for she was easily frightened in the night, so Odette lay in the darkness willing herself to be patient. How strange it was to think that the ritual of putting Celeste to bed had not changed over all the years. Each night she had tucked her sister into bed with the same words and caresses. That evening she and James had talked about the summer in Gaspé, and now she thought about that old white house in the middle of a field and another summer night when the fifteen-year-old version of herself was helping her sister, then eighteen, into her nightdress and watching over her as she said her prayers. And across the field in the other house James was in his bed; he was only fourteen then. Or had he been lying awake, kneeling by the little window in the attic, looking out across the field and thinking about her? He had told her again this evening how madly he was in love with her that summer. And now here he was, an elderly man, sleeping in his room in the big hotel and still thinking of her, maybe. Yes, he had been in love with her that summer, but she had been entranced by Gabriel the crippled boy. She and Celeste had shared a room in that farmhouse with Lucille and Sylvie, who lay there in their narrow bed farting and giggling, talking about Celeste, their simple sister, wondering when she would be able to talk properly and count to ten. What cruel little bitches they were! Odette felt a growing anger at the memory and knew it was crazy. It wouldn't help the headache that was threatening her, and anyway she'd had her revenge on those two. They didn't get a penny from her lottery win, nor would they in her will.

In only a few moments Celeste was sleeping. Odette could

hear the snores, and so she arose and went down the stairs carefully in the dark to the kitchen. There she took down the brandy bottle and poured a good measure. She added some water and slowly made her way up the stairs to her bedroom, stopping once to sip a little. Settled again into bed, she carefully placed the glass on the little side table. Already she felt better, and again she thought of Celeste and the stunted life she had led, trapped in her own diminished world. But still she got down each night on her arthritic knees, her hands raised upward, either to God or just black space. Did anyone know? But of course it was a matter not of knowing but of believing. Anyway, tomorrow would be a good day for Celeste. She was frail now and might not last much longer. Yet lying there, Odette could hardly imagine a life without Celeste.

The brandy was soothing. She thought again of Raoul in La Résidence, fuming and forgetful, seeing enemies everywhere, as full of rage as he'd always been, only now it was even more unpredictable. Such a contrast to James, who was a gentle man and educated, a former professor who had studied the works of poets and novelists all his life. He told her he was now reading Homer's *Odyssey*. A few pages every night before sleep. He said he had read the book every year for over half a century and told her that one day he would like to read it to her. He would explain the background to the story, and wouldn't it be great if they were together somehow and each night he could read a chapter to her? He remembered how as a young girl she had been curious and interested in words and reading. It was one of the things that attracted him. And that was true enough. He had ignited in her an interest in books, but nothing came of it, and when that summer was over, she returned to Montreal. A few years later she met Mr. Alphonse and began her life at the Green Mermaid, where she read almost nothing. Now and then she had glanced at a dirty book one of the other girls was reading. But poetry and stories of Greek legends were never a part of her life.

Now she had to wonder and had been wondering all week what James Hillyer saw in her. Why had he gone to the trouble of finding her after all those years? He'd known nothing about her winning that money, and anyway he was well off enough himself. She was just an uneducated woman who had spent most of her life directing cab traffic around the city for Dubé Taxi. By any measure, a fairly humble occupation. She was now no longer the beauty she had once been, although he said she was and had kissed her with feeling that night as she got into the taxi. Earlier he'd said he was still smitten by her and she had asked him about the word *smitten*, just as she had years ago whenever she didn't understand an English word. He told her it was from the verb *smite*, meaning to strike or hit, but in the past tense it meant the opposite of hurting. In other words he was still struck by her or infatuated or in love with her. Even after all those years. She couldn't quite believe that and asked him why. He said she was fishing for compliments and she said no, she was just curious. Then he said that curiosity had been one of the things he liked about her when she was fifteen. And then he said he also liked her vitality and her rough-edged sense of humour and her essential kindness. He told her he understood now how right she had been to scold him for his mean attitude towards Gabriel Fontaine, even though Gabriel sometimes was selfish and mean himself. She had told him then, all those years ago, that he had to learn how to forgive people who had serious handicaps like Gabriel. It hadn't made sense to him then, but now it did; now he could see how he should have listened to a fifteen-year-old girl who criticized him for not being a better friend to a crippled boy that summer. "I liked all that and of course your sexy brown legs." He'd told her all that this evening in the café on the Grande Allée, and it was something to hear those nice things. Especially after weeks and months of ill will and jealousy and accusations from members of her family and the disordered rage of poor Raoul. The brandy was calming her and the headache was receding. She began to feel sleepy and thought of a holiday with James. Perhaps they could go away together and get to know one another even better. She could take Celeste, who would enjoy that. It was a comforting thought that eased her finally into sleep.

• •

The next morning they visited the island in the little rented Honda. She sat beside James and, glancing now and then at the road map, directed him towards the bridge that led to Route 368, which circled the island. In the back seat Celeste gazed out at the fields, shy in the company of a stranger. She hadn't said a word since getting into the car. But James was friendly, and when he gave her a smile, she returned it. Odette remarked on the beauty of the summer day and all three looked out from time to time at the sky now filled with large white clouds, which sometimes obscured the sun and spread huge shadows across the green fields on either side of the road. Odette was delighted by the perfection of the day as they passed through the island's villages, Sainte Pétronille, Saint Laurent, and Saint Jean, and farther along Sainte Famille and Saint François.

In the late morning they stopped at a service centre where

Odette took her sister to a toilet and James too took advantage of the stop. A few miles on they spotted a picnic table by the road-side and stopped for lunch, with Odette spreading a red-and-white-checkered tablecloth and laying out tuna salad sandwiches and pickles and an apple pie. She also opened a bottle of red wine, though James was careful to have only one glass. Odette poured another for her sister, who drank it quickly. "Only one more after that," said Odette. "Alcohol goes to her head easily," she ex-plained to James in English. Odette herself had three glasses and declared that this Wednesday was one of the best she'd had in months. James too was enjoying himself and told her that com-ing to Quebec was one of the best things he had ever done. After they cleaned up and put everything in the garbage pail, they set out for Ste. Anne de Beaupré. As they drove, Odette pointed ahead at the foothills of the Laurentians. She said she was glad that they had their lunch earlier because the sky had now clouded over and a few drops of rain were spattering the windshield. But the sky fooled them, for as they neared the town, the sunlight broke forth again and they all felt better in this brighter world as the big church came into view. Now Celeste was animated and eager to see again the crutches and canes, mute testimony of God's powerful mercy toward the crippled believers.

In the big church, Celeste stood transfixed before them and then walked slowly to a pew near the back, where she knelt to pray. Odette watched her carefully and then took James's hand as they walked up the aisle. Halfway she stopped suddenly and tightened her grip in his. When he glanced at her, she seemed frozen standing there halfway up the church aisle. "What is it?" he whispered. "Let's sit down," she said, and they moved into a row of empty pews. She looked back to see Celeste, who was staring up at the church's ceiling. Then Odette leaned her head against the pew in front of her. To James, she looked stricken. "What is it, Odette? Please!"

"I think," she said, "that's Raoul up near the front."

He looked ahead and saw the back of a large man in a grey suit coat on his knees. "Why would you think that?" he whispered.

"I don't know," she said, still leaning against the pew.

"You're trembling," and he took her hand again. "Try to relax. Why would he be here on the very day that we are?"

"He was wandering the streets yesterday," she said, "and the police picked him up. He did something in a phone booth. I didn't want to tell you. I didn't want to spoil this day."

"But they must have returned him to that home."

"I hope so."

"You're letting your imagination get the better of you."

She was looking sideways at him as she spoke. "He could have come on one of the tour buses," she said. "I don't want him to see us here. I'm going back to the car. I don't want him to see Celeste either." James too was now resting his brow against a pew as they whispered together.

"You're not making sense."

"Maybe, but I'm not taking any chances. I should have told you about the police picking him up yesterday. I'm sorry."

"But would he pray like that? Is he religious?" James looked up again at the broad-backed grey suit.

"Yes," she said. "In his own way he is religious. You wouldn't think it from the life he has led. All that stealing and beating up people. In and out of jail. But he still goes to church and prays."

"But why would he be here on the very day that we are? It's too much of a coincidence."

She shook her head. "I don't know, James. But I'm going to the car before he turns around and comes down that aisle. He's so unpredictable. You just never know what he's going to do. I'm going to the car now and I'm taking Celeste. But please stay here until we're out of the church. I don't want him to see us together." She glanced up again before leaving, but all she saw in the third or fourth row was the big man's back.

Five minutes after she left the church, she watched James walking to the car. When he opened the door, he shrugged his shoulders. They were parked so they could see those coming out, but far enough away not to be noticed. Odette seemed calmer now. "Those tourists will be going soon," she said. "These tour buses have a schedule to keep. We'll just wait and see." More tourists were now streaming from the church as rain began to spatter the windshield.

James started the car and set the wipers going. "He could be just some guy coming to the church to pray," he said.

"We'll see," said Odette, and they watched the tourists now hurrying through the shower to the bus. The big man in the grey suit appeared talking to a couple and smiling. And Odette said, "No, it's not Raoul. It's just another big man." Leaning over, she kissed James on the cheek. "I'm sorry, James. I panicked there."

"It's okay," he said, "but you have to get this Raoul out of your head."

"Yes, I know you're right. I got a bit carried away, didn't I?" She reached back and grasped her sister's hand. "I'm sorry, Celeste, I just thought I saw someone I knew in there."

"Was Raoul in the church, Odette?"

"No, he wasn't. I just mistook someone for him. Do you want to go back into the church?"

"It's all right. I have sent my prayers to Sainte Anne. Everything will be fine."

"That's good."

They pulled out of the parking lot and were on their way back to the city. Everyone was silent until Odette said, "I've been thinking, James. Could you come to dinner tomorrow? About five o'clock? I want to treat you. It won't be as good as last night's dinner, but I think it will be all right. Do you like fish? Fresh fish? Or maybe I could make a tourtière."

"I've never had that," he said. "But I love fresh fish. It's hard to get sometimes in Toronto. I'll bring a bottle of wine."

"No, don't bring anything but yourself." She sounded better now. She'd regained her spirit, and when he glanced at her, she was looking out the window at the countryside. "Yes," she said. "We'll have a little celebration of our meeting again after all those years." She shook her head. "I can't believe I acted so silly back in that church."

"It's all right," he said. "Don't worry about it. A little attack of nerves. Nothing serious."

She smiled at him. "Yes, you're right. A little attack of nerves. Do you know, James, you are a very nice man. I wouldn't have thought you'd turn out this way years ago when you were a kid. You sounded so superior to everyone then. You seemed to have no kindness in you."

"Maybe," he said. "I was a bit of a spoiled brat, I think. Private school and all that. I had to learn how life sometimes treats us. I lost my wife and daughter. It taught me something. I'm still not sure what. Humility? Compassion? Maybe understanding others a little more."

She had her hand on his thigh. "Yes, yes, death will do that.

I remember when my brother Maurice died. He was my favourite brother. He turned bad, poor Maurice. Got in with the wrong people. Joined this gang and began to rob banks. He was killed up in your part of the world. In Toronto. Shot by the police after a holdup. Do you remember him at all from when you were down in Gaspé?"

"Well, yes, I read that in the paper. About him being killed, I mean. This was back in the sixties, right?"

"Yes, in 1963. Near the end of that summer in Gaspé you gave him a model airplane."

"Yes, I think I remember that."

"He was only thirteen then and he thought you wanted him to put it together for you."

"Did he? My memory of that is vague, but yes. Was that the evening we walked together in the field behind your house? It was near the end of the summer and you were angry with me because I was ignoring Gabriel. I wasn't being friends with him. There was a moon that night. A big full moon rising out of the sea. An incredible sight. And you were so mad at me. Said things that hurt. I think I went back to the house and cried all night. What a baby I was!"

"I don't remember that. I don't remember any moon, but I was cross with you a lot. A stuck-up kid with no heart. That's how I would have described you. But then what am I saying? Even then you had kindness in you. You gave me that money when I told you I was pregnant." She was looking again out the side window. "I think I misjudged you. What do we know at that age, eh? Fourteen? Fifteen? We know nothing about life at all."

"Yes," he said. "Not much."

"It took me so long to learn things. I wasted so much time on worthless men. Too much booze probably. And I'm still at it though not as bad, I think. Only you and Marcel Dubé were good to me. And look, it's taken so long for you to find me. Where have you been all these years, you old scoundrel?" She kissed his cheek again.

"Whoa. Easy now." A car passing them tooted its horn and the couple in the front seat waved cheerfully. Odette looked back now at her sister, who was staring out her window. She always looked a little sad, unless she was watching cartoons. "We were just having a little joke, Celeste," she said in French. "I've invited James to have dinner with us tomorrow. I think I'll make something special. Would you like that?"

"Yes, I would, Odette."

"We'll have a little party, you and James and me. I am going to teach him some French so he can have a conversation with you."

"Thank you," she said in her solemn manner.

Now she was trying to remember that night. Poor Maurice. Just a kid then. She could never have imagined that he would become a criminal.

• •

August 1944

We were walking through the hayfield towards her house. With the sun down, the air was already cool. There were lights now in village houses. In another field, a cow was bawling for her calf, which must have strayed. Suddenly Odette was running ahead of me, holding the model plane aloft, shouting as she ran. Maurice Huard, his hands deep in his pockets, was standing on the gallery watching his sister. Odette then threw the little airplane and we watched it soar briefly through the darkening air and fall to the ground. When I caught up to her, Odette was bent over, breathing hard and laughing.

"I smoke too much, I think," she said. "I can't run anymore."

Maurice had jumped down from the gallery and run over to get the airplane.

"What were you saying to your brother?" I asked.

"I said the airplane was a gift from you. I also told him he was a donkey. Come on, let's go for a walk before it gets too dark. Let's go up in the field. Now that they've cut the hay."

We walked up the sloping field towards the brow of the hill, where cattle were grazing on the other side of the fence. From there we could see down to the houses in the village with their lighted windows, and the road and the bay. There was little traffic on the road. Few people in the village had a car, and the tourists were now in their cabins and motor courts. Odette and I stood by the fence looking down at it all. Behind us the heavy dark shapes of animals were moving; you could hear them cropping the grass and shitting. Odette and I seemed awkward with one another. Finally she said, "Gabriel wonders why you have been away all week. He misses you."

"I'm browned off with him," I said. "All that stuff at the picnic. When the guy picked him up. Gabriel was crazy, acting the way he did. Nuts. A little kid wouldn't have carried on like he did."

Odette spoke very softly.

"Gabriel doesn't like to be touched. You know that, James. And that son-of-a-whore Emile didn't even ask. He just picked up

Gabriel like he was a bag of potatoes or something. And carried him off. It was a stupid thing to do. Gabriel is proud. You know that."

"So we all stand around in the rain because he's proud."

"We'd have got him out in his wheelchair, the four of us. With a little more time and patience we could have done it. With someone like Gabriel, you have to be patient. The boy is crippled. He'll never walk again. Just imagine that! He'll never do what we're doing right now. Walking up in this field and looking out at all this as if it's nothing. We can do this every day. Just think about him in that wheelchair. He's proud and he's hurt because you haven't been around to see him all week. You're supposed to be his friend."

I'd heard all this before.

"Gabriel," I said, "is a pain in the ass. A spoiled rich brat."

"You always say that, don't you? And you? What are you? A fucking sorehead. Yes, that's what you are. Young Mister Sorehead who spends all day up in his room playing with himself, I bet."

I walked away from her then, striding down the hill. I imagine I was close to tears. After a while I heard her behind me running to catch up. Grabbing me by the arm.

"I'm sorry I said that. It was stupid. I can be stupid. Stop and listen to me now."

She had pulled me to a halt and we stood there looking at each other.

"I like you, James, and I want to be your friend. Don't be sore at me, okay? I'm sorry I said that."

I felt the grip of her hand on my arm, smelled her faintly sour breath. I was mortified by everything, choked up with humiliation and the rawest, most vulnerable love for this girl.

"I'll go to Percé tomorrow and see him," I croaked.

She linked her arm in mine and we began again to walk down

the field among the haycocks, both of us embarrassed by all the feeling that had been laid bare between us. Then she cried, "Look." She was pointing at an enormous orange moon that was rising out of the sea, flooding the bay with light. We stopped to watch its rising.

"It's a big bugger, isn't it?" she said. "Just look at that."

And it was something to behold, a luminous, elemental presence, governing tidal waters, arresting thought, filling us both with a momentary wonder.

Raoul

Âfter climbing the verandah steps, he put down the suitcase. He felt good, pleased at how it all had worked out. Only an hour ago he had thought that finding the house would be difficult; he would get a taxi driver who would be a smartass when he told him that he didn't know the name of the street he wanted. But the young guy only said, "Anything in particular you remember about the street, sir? A church or something?" He told him then about the flower garden and the big park across the street from the house. He said he couldn't recall the name of the street or the number of the house, but he remembered the park. He said he was now in his eighties and sometimes had trouble with his memory.

"That's all right, sir," the young guy said. "My father has a problem with his memory too and he's only in his sixties.

Sixty-eight now, I think." He had already put the car in gear and they were on their way. "I think the park you mentioned is the Plains of Abraham and the street you want is probably Laurier. It's not far. Will you recognize the house if you see it?"

"For sure, I will," Raoul said. What a nice young guy he was. Why weren't there more people in the world like him?

They sped along the Grande Allée and then turned right on Montcalm and right again on Laurier. "Do you see the house you want?" the driver asked, and miraculously there it was.

"Yes," he said. "That red brick one with the white verandah."

They got out and the driver took the suitcase from the trunk while Raoul counted the change in his pocket. There wasn't much left; in fact, he was fifty cents short. He had thought to give the guy a big tip. He looked at the coins in his hand and gave them to the driver. "I think I'm a little short."

The young man counted the money and shrugged. "Don't worry about it, sir. Have a nice day."

Raoul couldn't fathom such kindness, it didn't seem real to him, but he said finally, "You too." But the door had closed by then and the taxi was on its way. Now on the verandah it occurred to him that perhaps a wonderful thing had happened; why could that young man not have been an angel sent by God to deliver him here without an argument? An angel who had wished him a good day even though he was fifty cents short on the fare? God moves in mysterious ways, his wonders to perform. He had heard that saying once and had written it down on a piece of paper and memorized it because it made good sense. He was meant to live in this house with his wife and sister-in-law. He couldn't remember feeling better about life, and peering through the oval-shaped glass in the front window, he pressed the doorbell. He thought he heard music. It was probably Celeste and her cartoons. An old woman now, but still living in a child's head. But Celeste liked him and she was always polite. A friend, really. Perhaps his only friend. Looking again through the glass, he wondered where Odette was. He knew she didn't like loud music. She had never liked loud music. It was funny the things you remembered and that was one of them. When they lived together, she was always telling him to turn down the radio or television. It used to irritate the hell out of him, but she told him once that while working at the Green Mermaid, she'd heard enough loud music to last her a lifetime. She was right, in a way. It was a noisy place and sometimes the music got on his nerves too and he'd go outside for a cigarette in the parking lot. Now he looked through the glass again. Odette had to be out of the house. She would never put up with that noise. But perhaps it was a good thing that she wasn't around. He could put his clothes away. Find a cupboard and closet and dresser drawers and arrange his shirts and underwear and socks. Make everything nice and tidy. She'd like that. He would surprise her when he opened the closet doors and showed her how everything was in order. She would find out too how useful he could be to have around. He could mow the grass, though it looked freshly cut when he'd got out of the taxi. She must pay someone to do that. But that was something he could do. Or he could help with the cleaning. There were lots of things he could do to help her.

He continued to press the bell until he saw Celeste turning from the stairs to hurry along the hallway towards him. Instinctively he put his face against the glass and with his thumbs in his ears, wiggled his fingers. It was an old joke between them, and by then she was laughing at his mashed nose and crossed eyes. On the other side of the glass she said between giggles, "Odette told me not to let anyone in the house, Raoul."

"But it's me, Celeste. I am coming to live with you and Odette. Didn't she tell you?"

Again he made his funny face, but now she only looked puzzled. "See," he said, "I brought my things in this suitcase. Listen to me now, my girl. I want to be with you. I want us to say our prayers together." Pointing upward, he said, "I want to speak to God with you." Celeste looked blankly at him through the glass. What if he had come all this way and she wouldn't let him in? Her look made him uneasy, sparking an irritant as old and familiar as his two hands. An overheated teakettle with its spout whistling. Someone once described him that way. Who was that? And crazily enough, he could remember. A guard at Bordeaux. A red-haired guy with a big laugh who used to call him Teakettle Cloutier because of his short temper. The nickname stuck with him, and in a way he didn't mind. One day years later on a street in Drummondville—was it Drummondville? he wasn't sure—an old con he didn't recognize passed him on the street and then stopped and called back, "Hey, Teakettle, how is it going?" They had a little talk there on the street. Having a nickname wasn't so bad. You carried something along with the name. A certain reputation. So now he had to keep the lid on the kettle. "We'll watch your shows on the television together, Celeste," he said. "I phoned Odette and she said it was all right to let me in."

On the other side of the glass she still looked puzzled. The poor woman didn't get much company. Cooped up in this big house all day. He would be a companion for her, and that was another thing he could do if he lived here. Teach her to play cribbage or something. Give Odette a chance to get out by herself while he looked after her sister. He hoped he could remember to tell her that. He could take Celeste out for walks too. See the city. Go to a movie or something. It was a good idea any way you looked at it.

To his relief, she was now unlocking the door, and after setting down his suitcase inside, he gave her a hug. How thin and bony the poor creature was. How much time did she have left anyway? She wasn't as old as him, he didn't think, but then he was no longer sure just how old he was. It didn't matter. Fuck it! He was now in his house and he hugged her again. "I'm going to take this suitcase up the stairs to my room, Celeste. Where is Odette, my girl?"

"She went to the grocery store, Raoul. She had to buy food for tonight. We're having James for dinner with us. She'll be home soon. She left right after lunch."

He had stopped on the first step of the stairs and set down his bag. He was frowning at her. "James? Who is James?"

"He's Odette's friend. James is from Ontario. He cannot speak French."

Raoul again felt the approach of something but reminded himself to stay calm. Breathe deeply and not upset himself. "He's not staying here, is he, Celeste? Not sleeping with Odette?"

"No. He's staying at the big hotel down by the river. Yesterday he took us in his car to Ste. Anne de Beaupré. Odette thought she saw you there in the big church."

"She did, eh?" He was trying to stay calm. What was the word the shrink used in Donnacona? *Agitation*. Yes. He must not get like that. All excited and nervous. A fancy word for being pissed off. He mustn't get upset. He gripped the handle of the old suitcase. "After I take this upstairs, you and I are going to have a game of hide-and-go-seek. What do you say to that?"

She clapped her hands. "It's my favourite game."

"I know it is," he said, and turned towards the stairs.

The racket was coming from Celeste's room. He turned off the television and stood by the doorway to Odette's room with its neatly made bed. That was where he really belonged. Where he should be sleeping with his wife, as any married man would. And maybe they could still do some other things in that bed. Was that not his lawful right? The things they used to do. She was hungry for it all the time when they were younger. She couldn't keep her hands off him. Maybe they could do that again. Why not? He carried his bag along the hallway to a small room that overlooked the lawn and garden at the back of the house. This room would do until they talked about their new life together over a glass of beer or wine. He had no money to buy beer or wine but he would get his pension cheque at the end of the month. Meantime she had plenty. Monique had said twelve million but he couldn't imagine such a sum. But this was all going to be fine; he would make it work. He knew one thing for sure. He never wanted to see the inside of that old people's home again and nobody was going to make him.

He went back downstairs and into the kitchen, where Celeste was waiting for their game to begin. "Celeste," he said, "I have to call my sister."

Celeste nodded. "I just remembered. Your sister called. She wants Odette to phone her back."

"All right. Why don't you go and hide? Find a good place.

Give me a few minutes to talk to Monique and then I'll try to find you. How does that sound?"

"Okay. You have to turn to the wall and close your eyes so you don't see where I'm going."

"Sure thing. Here I go."

After she left, he called Monique's number and she answered right away as if she had been sitting by the phone waiting for it to ring. "Where are you, Raoul? I was going to call the police again, but I don't want to bother them so much. I think they're getting a little fed up with me calling about you. The people at La Résidence phoned about noon. They hadn't noticed you were gone until then."

He laughed, pleased with this news. He had fooled them for sure. Stupid as pig shit they were. "Listen, Monique. I used the oldest trick in the world to get out. Rolled up some sheets and pillows and made it look like I was still in bed sleeping. Guys at Donnacona used to do that. Then I went out the back way. Down the stairs to the basement and out a window in the furnace room. That was at five o'clock this morning. Nobody around. Then I walked to the bus stop. I had the number of the bus written on a piece of paper. I had it all written down. Your brother isn't as stupid as you think he is."

"I've never called you stupid. But listen, let me talk to Odette."

"She's not here right now. She's out shopping for dinner. She's got a boyfriend now and he's coming for dinner. But listen. After the bus ride, I got a taxi and he brought me right to the door. I didn't even know the name of the street or the number of the house, but he got me here anyway. And something else. I didn't have enough money to pay my fare, but he said that was all right. I was fifty cents short, but it didn't matter to the driver. Now how many taxi drivers would you find who would do something like that? I'm telling you, Monique, I think the driver, just a young guy, was an angel, a real angel sent by God to deliver me to this house."

"An angel, Raoul? What on earth are you talking about?"

"I'm talking about an angel who brought me to this house."

"Raoul, I don't think Odette wants you in her house."

"Our house, Monique," he said. "This big house is half mine. I'm her husband."

"Listen, Raoul, I talked to Madame Fournier at La Résidence and she told me you will not be allowed back into that facility. Now we have to find another place for you."

"I have found my place, goddamn it, and it's right here where I'm standing. Can't you understand that, little sister?"

"The people at the home said they could no longer accept responsibility for your care."

"So what? Fuck them. I'm staying here."

"Please don't use that kind of language. You're going to get into trouble."

"Not at all. Odette and Celeste and me are going to have a nice dinner tonight and everything will be fine."

"I think the police are getting tired of looking for you when you run off like this."

"No reason now for them to look for me. I don't want any more trouble with the cops. I've had enough trouble with them in my lifetime. Right now I'm playing a game with Celeste. She likes her games. I'm going to help Odette look after her sister. You'll see."

"Are you sure you're not going to stir up trouble? What

about this man who is also coming to dinner? You didn't mention him. What are you going to do about him? Throw him out of the house? How do you think Odette would like that?"

"I'm not throwing anybody out of my house. He can have his dinner and then it will be time for him to go. No trouble, Monique. I've had enough trouble in my life."

"You're telling me. Have Odette phone me when she gets back."

"Sure. I'll do that, Monique. Don't worry."

" 'Don't worry, Monique.' If only it were that simple, Raoul. I just don't think you understand." And she hung up.

It was only the afternoon but already he was tired. His knees and hips ached as he climbed the stairs. Lugging that damn suitcase to the bus stop, an old man in jeans and the jacket from his suit. Christ, he must have bought that suit thirty-five years ago. Now here he was, playing a game with a simple-minded woman. He always knew where to find her. She would be in her closet crouching behind dresses and nightgowns. Then from below, he heard a door opening and Odette calling, "Celeste? I'm back. Where are you? Are you upstairs?"

He opened the closet door and Celeste slid by him without a word and made her way slowly down the stairs. "I'm here, Odette. I'm coming down," she cried.

At the top of the stairs, he stood watching Celeste holding on to the banister with one hand as she slowly descended. Then he saw Odette at the bottom of the stairway looking up past her sister at him. She was holding two bags of groceries and frowning.

Odette

She was looking up at him with disbelief. "What the hell are you doing here, Raoul? How did you get in my house?" He was now coming down the stairs towards her, his knees aching with each step.

"I let him in, Odette," said Celeste. "It's just Raoul. It's all right, isn't it?"

"No, it's not all right, Celeste, goddamn it." She was shaking her head as she carried the groceries into the kitchen and put the bags on the counter near the fridge.

Celeste had begun to cry. "I'm sorry, Odette." She looked like misery itself, weeping at the kitchen table, and Odette felt like saying something to her, but then Raoul was in the kitchen filling the doorway.

"Why are you here?" she asked. "I thought I made it clear

that I don't want you in my house again. We are finished, Raoul. And we have been for years. For God's sake, try to understand that."

His blank stare was incomprehensible, the look of a man who might do anything. Shaking her head again, she began to put away the groceries, opening cupboard doors. Concentrate. Stay busy, she reminded herself.

"Can I help you with anything?" he asked.

She stopped putting things away and turned to him. She was holding a can of tomatoes and could easily have thrown it across the room at him. But she only said, "Yes, you could help me. You could make my life easier by just leaving the house. I'll give you money for the taxi."

He smiled then and said, "I came here by taxi from the bus stop, and this young driver was so good to me. I didn't even have enough money, but that was okay with him. He told me not to worry about it. So help me, Odette, I believe I was delivered here by an angel from God. I really do. I was brought here to help you and your sister in this big house."

Dear God, an angel, she thought. What next? She had to call Monique and get all this straightened out. She'd phone James too and tell him not to bother coming. With Raoul here it was too complicated. Somehow she had to calm down. Control herself. She needed a drink, damn it. If she had a quick brandy, she could get on with the telephone calls. But she had to get the both of them out of the kitchen. Crossing the room she sat down beside her sister and took her hand. She even managed a feeble smile at Raoul, who was still standing by the doorway. "I'm sorry I yelled at you, Celeste. I didn't mean it."

"That's all right, Odette. I know you didn't mean it."

"Look, will you do me a favour?"

"Yes, I will. What do you want me to do?"

"Well, it isn't very hard. I just want you and Raoul to go upstairs and watch some television. I need a few moments to myself."

"Sure. Of course, we can do that." She looked back at Raoul. "Can't we, Raoul?"

"Why not?" he said. "Fine by me."

"That's good then," said Odette, getting up as they walked out to the hallway and up the stairs. Soon she heard the television, and went to the back porch and poured a couple of inches of brandy into a mug that belonged to her sister. Looking at Mickey Mouse's face made her feel a bit silly. Why was she drinking from the damn thing? Why had she picked it up? Was she going a little crazy too? She had to control herself. She shouldn't have yelled at Celeste. She must keep everything on a quieter level and above all avoid confrontation. Was that the word? Yes, confrontation. It would be difficult, but she would do it. She had to do it. It was this disease he had. It shrank the brain or something. You can't get into an argument with someone like that. The brandy was calming her, and now she could hear laughter from Celeste's room. Raoul was good to her. Perhaps it was because with her he never encountered opposition. They got on well together and he now seemed to be okay. Still, getting him out of the house would be difficult, so perhaps it would be better if she left things until tomorrow. She thought again of phoning James, telling him that Raoul was here, and asking him if he still wanted to come. He might say no, and she so wanted to see him. She wanted him to be there, and perhaps it would be a good thing if Raoul saw that she had moved on in another direction. Away from him. But she almost laughed. She was kidding herself if she believed that. He would never accept it. And never change. It was frustrating not to know what to do. In the back porch, she poured herself another inch or two of brandy and drank it quickly. Felt her nerves steadying as she went back to the kitchen and, after preparing a glaze, put the ham in the oven. None of the fish in the store looked fresh enough, so she had settled on the ham. It was nearly four o'clock. She had time for a shower and a change of clothes and then she would get on with dinner. Chill some wine. Peel some potatoes and carrots. Make a salad. Try at least to pretend that everything was normal. She was having a small dinner party and she would treat Raoul like any guest and the same with James. Try not to show him any affection. Just a friend. She would have to put a good face on things and try to be hopeful. After James left, she would make up the bed in the back room for Raoul. Keep him happy at least for the night. It was a better plan than trying to get him out of the house this evening. She had put some beer and wine in the fridge. Before dinner she'd give Raoul a beer, but no liquor. Maybe a glass or two of wine for dinner. In the morning while he was upstairs she would call the police to get him out of the house. James had told her that she might need a legal document for this. What was it called? It would allow the police to arrest Raoul if he disobeyed the court order. What was it called? She would ask James again when they had a moment together. She would have to get a lawyer, but it would be worth it.

   She was about to phone Raoul's sister when the ringing phone startled her. "Odette? It's Monique. How is it going? Is Raoul behaving himself?"

"He's okay right now. He and Celeste are watching TV. How did you know he was here?"

"He phoned a while ago and sounded a little strange. Said he was driven there by an angel. Maybe he was kidding, I don't know."

"Well, Celeste let him in and he seems okay. For now."

"Has he told you how he got out of La Résidence this morning?"

"No."

"He put some blankets and things on his bed to make it look like he was sleeping and then slipped out a window in the basement, though with the size of him, I don't know how he managed that. This was at five o'clock this morning."

"God Almighty."

"He took a bus into the city and then a taxi to your place. He couldn't remember your street or the number of your house, but he said the driver helped him, and that's when he started going on about angels. By the way, Madame Fournier phoned at noon to tell me that Raoul can no longer stay at La Résidence. He needs a special kind of care that they don't provide. She wants us to come around and get the rest of his things. I don't know what to do with him, Odette."

"Well, you will have to put him in a place with better security. He's not going to like it, but you haven't any choice. He can stay here tonight. Getting him out today would be too complicated. He'd make a fuss and I don't need that. I'm having a little dinner party this evening. A friend from Ontario is coming."

"Yes. Raoul mentioned it."

"I'll make up a bed for Raoul in the back room. It would be just too complicated to get him out of the house tonight."

"You are doing the right thing, Odette. Keep him calm. That is the main thing. Let me call the police in the morning for you. I'll explain things, though they mostly know all about him now. We don't want him to overhear you calling them. It will only upset him."

"Thank you, Monique."

"I'll call them around nine o'clock. Try to keep him away from the front door around nine and get the police in the house before he knows it, if you can."

"Yes."

"You're not worried that he will be upset with your male friend there? You know how possessive he can be. In his own way the poor man still loves you."

"I know he is terribly jealous. Always has been, but I'm taking a chance that James's presence won't upset him and, since I'm letting him sleep here tonight, he will not see James as some kind of rival. But it's a bit of a gamble, I know. I'll try to make it work. James will understand. He is an educated man, a retired university professor, and I've told him about my life with Raoul, so he will know what to expect. It's funny but it just came to me. That legal thing you need to keep a person out of your house. It's called a restraining order. I should have had that done before. Thank you again for calling the police tomorrow. And somehow we'll get through this evening."

"Well, try not to upset him. He still loves you."

"No, he doesn't. I'm sorry but you're wrong about that, Monique. Your brother doesn't love me or anyone else. Not even my poor sister, who is really only someone he can manipulate. Raoul has never loved me. He's incapable of love because he cannot tolerate anything but absolute obedience to his wishes or opinions. A person like that doesn't really know what love is."

"Well, maybe you're right. Our father was like that too. A strange and difficult man. But Raoul is still my brother and I love him. Please don't get him angry."

"God, no."

"And tell your friend."

"Oh, James won't provoke him in any way. I have to go now, Monique."

"Good luck with your dinner."

"Yes. Thanks."

With the ham in the oven, she peeled the potatoes and washed the carrots. She would make a salad later. In a way she was already regretting her invitation. She should have suggested a restaurant. She had never been much of a cook. When she lived with Raoul, she put together quick meals of hamburg steak and potatoes or macaroni and cheese and he never complained as long as there was plenty of it. When she lived alone, she often ate out, sometimes with Marcel. They had favoured a Chinese restaurant on rue Ste. Catherine. When she rescued Celeste from her sisters and they lived together in St. Henri, she was back to simple meals and Celeste never complained.

She heard the footsteps on the stairs, and then Raoul came into the kitchen and sat down at the table. "You wouldn't have a beer in the house, would you, Odette?"

"Yes, of course. I'll get one for you," and she went to the fridge and, opening a beer, began to pour it into a glass.

"The bottle is okay," he said, and she set it on the table. "So this boyfriend of yours has come all the way from Ontario to see you, eh? He must have no worries about money."

"I wouldn't exactly call him a boyfriend."

"Is that so? What would you call him then?"

"He's just an old friend. We knew one another as kids. Teenagers. The summer we spent in Gaspé."

"Was he your first? They say women never get over the first one."

"Is that what they say, Raoul? Well, I don't know what you're talking about. We were just friends. He doesn't speak French, by the way, and since he's a guest, we'll be speaking English at dinner."

"Well, I can speak English too."

"I know you can. I just thought I'd tell you. I just didn't want you to feel . . ."

"Feel what?"

"I don't know. Out of place or something. I just want us to have a nice meal. We're speaking English as a courtesy."

"A courtesy, eh? Well, okay. I take it then that he's about your age."

"Yes. Actually I think he's a year younger."

"Robbing the cradle, are you?" and he laughed.

"I hope you won't . . ." and she stopped, warning herself about continuing this line of thought.

"Won't what? Fart at the dinner table? I'll try not to. Has he fucked you yet, or can he still do that? I can still do that, by the way."

"There you go. It's not necessary to talk like that."

He had finished his beer. "Can I have another of these?"

"There's one more in the fridge. We're having wine with dinner. I'll get the beer for you, but there isn't any more. Then I'm going upstairs for a bath."

"I don't suppose you want any company."

"Very funny, Raoul. Now if you'll excuse me."

He only shrugged.

Jesus, what a mess she had made of it. He was already getting under her skin. Goddamn his eyes. She was glad she'd hidden the brandy and the corkscrew. If he was going after the wine, he'd have to bite the top off, and she wouldn't put it past him. In her bedroom she phoned the hotel and got James. He told her he too was just about to take a bath himself. "Five-thirty, right?"

"Yes," she spoke softly. "I have to tell you, James. Something has come up. Raoul is here."

"I see. Would it be better if I didn't come then?"

"James, I want you to be here, but I thought I should tell you. He is so unpredictable. You just never know what you're going to get with Raoul. I just . . . I don't know."

"Are you in any danger? Do you feel threatened or anything?"

"Not really. I think I can handle the evening. It's just . . . I wanted you to know. I'm sorry, but Celeste let him in. He's going to be gone in the morning. But I want to keep the lid on things tonight. Do you still feel like coming?"

"Of course. But only if you want me to. I'll be there at five-thirty."

"Thank you, James."

James

In the taxi he looked out at people strolling along rue St. Louis and wondered what lay ahead for this summer evening. This Raoul Cloutier appeared to be a real handful for Odette, though he sensed that a part of her felt sorry for the man. Alzheimer's was hard to deal with, from what he'd read about it in newspapers and magazines, and he'd had a slight acquaintance with it in his last year of teaching when he watched a colleague, Jack Foster, a brilliant scholar in his prime, begin to lose his memory. As the disease enclosed him, he began to falter. At first, no one seemed to notice. But at meetings, during discussion, Jack sometimes appeared to lose track of his thoughts. He would apologize. Call it fatigue. He wasn't sleeping well, he used to say with a tired smile. Then someone told Hillyer that Jack was having trouble in his marriage. His second wife was a good deal younger and perhaps she couldn't handle the changes she saw in her husband. Within the year he was in a nursing home, put there by his first wife, who still cared for him. And Jack was only in his early seventies then. Something was there waiting for all of them in old age. But not, he hoped, dementia. What did old Lear say in his abject state in the storm on the heath? "O let me not be mad, not mad, sweet heaven / Keep me in temper; I would not be mad!" And now he was going to have dinner with this unpredictable Cloutier. Poor Odette. But was it not her kindness that was so evident, even though she no longer even liked the man? Perhaps she hadn't for years. But it was her nature to help people who seemed to need her. That summer in Gaspé she had looked after Gabriel Fontaine. Pushed that heavy old wooden wheelchair around the village. Shared his corny jokes and even gave her body to him, paying a terrible price. Later she looked after her sister. Yes, he thought. Everything has a price, even compassion.

The house on Avenue Wilfrid Laurier was quite handsome, and walking up the steps of the verandah, he thought, Good for you, Odette. After all those years in cold-water flats, you finally have a decent place to call home. It was obvious she had been watching for him because she opened the door immediately. He could hear the children's program from the television. Odette was dressed in another pantsuit and white blouse with the pearl necklace encircling her throat, though her eyes looked tired. After glancing back, she embraced him in the hallway, then kissed him hard. She smelled wonderful. "I'm glad you came," she whispered. "I need you here. He is upstairs now with Celeste. We'll eat in half an hour. Meantime we'll have a drink together at least. I've hidden the brandy. I don't want him getting into that. We'll have to watch the wine too, or he'll drink the whole damn bottle. I don't want to bring out another, so I've hidden it all away. But you and I can now have a Scotch in the living room. We're going to need one and anyway we deserve it."

They sat on the sofa while she poured them each a generous measure from the mickey of Dewar's. She added a little water and they quietly touched glasses.

"To us, James."

"To us."

"God, I'm glad you found me."

"Me too. I'm glad we found each other after all these years and you can see me now as something other than the righteous young know-it-all I was when we first met." She was drinking her Scotch quickly, and he put his hand on her arm. "Easy now."

"I'll be glad when this evening is over and Raoul can get the help he needs. Monique and Bertrand will find another place for him, I hope. I'll help them with the money. I suppose it's the least I can do. But I must find a lawyer and get that legal document that will keep the man from bothering me."

"That shouldn't be difficult." The whisky felt warm and comforting. He could have used another, and as if reading his mind, she poured some more into his glass. "Okay now," she whispered. "I'm putting this away so he won't find it, and then I'm going to get on with things in the kitchen. Care to join me?"

"Yes, of course. Lead the way. Is there anything I can do?"

"No, just finish your drink. I hate to rush you, but if he sees us drinking and can't have any, he could get ugly. The last thing I want in him tonight is whisky. He's never handled liquor well. I'll give him a couple of glasses of wine with dinner, but no more." She was tying an apron around her waist, and after taking the ham out of the oven, she began to make a gravy. Soon they heard Celeste and Raoul coming down the stairs. Celeste was laughing, probably at something Raoul said.

In the kitchen Raoul towered over James, who stood up. "So this is your new boyfriend, eh?"

"Raoul, this is James Hillyer from Toronto. He's just a friend."

Hillyer shook the enormous hand offered. Was it his imagination that the handshake was unnecessarily long and the grip mercilessly tight? "And you're a professor or something, aren't you?"

"Yes. Was. I've been retired now for several years."

But the big man wasn't listening; he had already turned his attention to Odette. "When do we eat, dear wife?"

"Soon." She was frowning at the stove. "I'm just going to slice the ham now. And Celeste. Can you set the table for me?" They were speaking French, but James could get the gist of things and asked, "Can I do anything?"

"No thanks. Everything is fine."

"Is there wine for dinner, dear wife?"

"Yes, Raoul. I'm going to open a bottle in a minute. And please don't call me that."

"Call you what?"

"What you have been calling me."

Raoul looked at James. "What is she talking about, Professor?"

But Odette spared him the effort of an awkward reply. "I'm talking about you calling me your dear wife."

"Well, I think I can call you what I feel like calling you in my own house."

"All right, all right, call me what you feel like calling me. Can you help Celeste set the table? And take in the bowl of salad."

"Of course I can, dear wife. I'd be glad to help Celeste," and he moved to the table and picked up the bowl and Odette made a wry face at Hillyer and returned to stirring the gravy at the stove. She already looked exasperated, and watching her, he wondered how many of these little squabbles had marked her time with Cloutier over the years. Hundreds probably. He supposed that many couples lived like this, with each taking part in inflicting small humiliations and snide remarks on the other. Mercifully he had been spared such a purgatorial marriage. Leah had been mostly good-natured, and while he had sometimes retreated into silence, even bad temper, it never lasted long. They'd had their differences but somehow they avoided outright argument; from their earliest days together it had been evident that both felt uneasy with discord.

He helped Odette take the food to the dining room, where Celeste and Raoul were already seated. Cloutier had removed his jacket and put it over the back of his chair. After rolling up his sleeves, he reached for the bowl of mashed potatoes. Celeste had bowed her head in silent prayer, and as they passed the food around, an uneasy silence descended over the room. The sound of cutlery seemed to slice the dead air. The wine was poured and hastily drunk by Cloutier. Celeste was picking delicately at her food, looking nervously at her sister as if she could feel the awkward and evident tension between Odette and Raoul. At the other end of the table Odette ate slowly, carefully, sipping her wine. The bottle was already half empty.

Raoul asked for more, and after his glass was filled, Odette made a point of emptying it by giving Celeste and James and herself another small pour. Cloutier had already finished his and smiled at James.

"So, how much do they charge you for a room in that big hotel?" he asked.

"Well, I'm staying a week and so they gave me a special price, though it's still fairly pricey."

"What do you mean by fairly pricey, Professor?"

"Oh, for God's sake, Raoul," said Odette. "What does it matter to you how much it is? It's expensive. All right?" With that she finished her glass of wine. It was as though he hadn't heard her.

"So, pricey would be what? A hundred dollars a night? Two hundred?"

"Nearly two hundred," James said.

"Two hundred dollars to sleep in a bed for one night. You must be rich, Professor."

"No, I'm not rich." He didn't know how to address this difficult man. "Raoul" seemed ridiculous and "Mr. Cloutier" not much better.

"What does a professor do for his paycheque? We had a visit once from a professor. In Donnacona. That's a place I was in a few years ago. They put me away for beating this guy in a fight. In court they told me I broke every bone in his face. The guy deserved it, but they wouldn't listen to me in that courtroom. Anyway, this professor gave us a speech about how to make use of our time there. We should read books, he said. That was years ago. I suppose he got a lot of money for that speech. I thought it was mostly bullshit."

"All right, Raoul," said Odette. "That's enough of that kind of language."

He looked down the table at her. "You think I'm vulgar, don't you, Odette? And maybe I am. But do you know what you are?"

"No, Raoul, what am I?"

"I'll tell you what you are, Odette. You're a slut. A little married slut and one day you are going straight to hell."

In the weeks and months that followed, Hillyer would often try to reassemble the parts of that summer evening that ended so chaotically. As he remembered it, Odette and Celeste sat at each end of the table and he and Cloutier were across from each other in the middle. Behind him was the handsome walnut china cabinet that Odette loved so much. She told him she'd fallen in love with it the moment she'd set eyes on it, in a furniture store on rue St. Jean. In trying to remember it all, he was fairly certain that the flashpoint of the evening had been Cloutier's use of the word *slut*, for he could remember saying, "You shouldn't call Odette that."

Cloutier was leaning forward, his elbows on the table. He knocked over his empty wineglass and was looking straight down the table at Odette. But after Hillyer's words, he suddenly got to his feet, knocking his chair backwards and glaring at Hillyer.

"Don't tell me what to say in my own house, mister. Have you fucked my wife yet, you little bastard?"

Then Odette too was standing up, after throwing her napkin on the table.

"That's enough," she cried. "I've had enough of you and your dirty mouth. I want you out of the house and I'm calling the police to see that it's done. No more. You're getting out."

"You're not calling the police, by God," he said. "You touch that phone and I'll break your neck."

Was Celeste crying by then? Yes, he thought so, but he couldn't be sure. He couldn't be sure of anything that happened in the next few minutes. When he stood up to follow Odette to the kitchen, he received a terrible blow across the face. It knocked him backwards against the china cabinet, and his head must have struck a corner of that cabinet because he found himself on the floor a moment later with his ears ringing. He could hear Odette's screams but only faintly. And there seemed to be glass in his hair. He must have been sitting up by then because he could remember looking down at the blood spilling from his nose. He hadn't seen so much of his own blood in decades: a childhood fall from an apple tree in the backyard of his home on Crescent Road in Toronto.

Then he heard shouting from the kitchen and Celeste's panic-stricken voice.

"You're hurting Odette, Raoul. You're hurting my sister. Let her go."

On his hands and knees, he had been helpless there in the dining room, and he felt the shame of his helplessness. When he tried a second time to get to his feet, he lost consciousness again and sometime later awakened to a young woman speaking to him in French. Asking for his name and address. Behind her a young man. Both were in uniform. Police? Paramedics? He could not tell, but the house seemed full of people, and when they carried him out on the stretcher, he saw Odette's neighbours standing on their lawns and verandahs in the evening dusk amid the revolving lights of the police cruisers and ambulances. But where was Odette and her sister and Cloutier?

Later at the hospital, when his mind had cleared, they told him that Madame Huard had survived the assault but might have suffered a heart attack, so she had been taken to intensive care. Her sister was with her. They did not mention Cloutier as they wheeled Hillyer into a room for observation.

Celeste

The policewoman *was very nice* and said not to worry, to just tell her what had happened in the house that evening. Celeste clutched her rosary. Thank God she had remembered it when the police came to take her away. So she touched the beads in the hospital and told the policewoman about Raoul and how angry he became at dinner. How he had knocked down Odette's friend from Ontario. Then she said that Raoul had followed Odette into the kitchen and was choking her on the floor. He had already broken her beautiful pearl necklace. She had begged Raoul to stop but he wouldn't, so she took the big knife from the kitchen counter and stabbed Raoul in the neck and all that blood came out. It was terrible and Raoul had groaned and his eyes seemed to go back into his head. But he had stopped choking Odette and just lay there on the floor beside her. Celeste told the policewoman how sorry she was to have done this to Raoul, but she was afraid for her sister's life. She liked Raoul and thought he was her friend, but he was hurting her sister and she had to do something.

Then she cried and the policewoman gave her some tissues to blow her nose and she told the policewoman she was afraid they would put her in jail. She didn't think she could live in jail at her age. The policewoman told her not to worry about that now. "You saved your sister's life," she said, "and the court will deal fairly with you, madame. We do not believe you are a risk to run away, and so you can stay with your sister until she recovers. We have arranged all this with the hospital." Yet it still bothered her that she had killed Raoul. She had plunged that knife into his neck and watched the blood staining the floor and Raoul weakening as he died. But she'd had to do something, and she hoped the policewoman was right and the court people would understand. How she wanted to see a priest and go to confession! She hoped that God would listen and understand and forgive her. Her rosary had been a comfort in her talk with the policewoman. And best of all, the hospital people told her that Odette was not going to die and leave her all alone in the world. That was all that really mattered now.

Aftermath

I n late *July, James and Odette* travelled by train to Percé and
stayed at the St. Lawrence Hotel, where Odette had once
worked as a chambermaid and James had spent many afternoons with Gabriel Fontaine all those years ago. Celeste did
not accompany them. In the days following Raoul Cloutier's assault on her sister, she became despondent, constantly worrying
about her picture in the paper and, in dark moments alone, fear-
ing that God would not absolve her for taking a life in violation
of the Sixth Commandment. Despite encouraging words from
Odette and even from neighbours who praised her courage in
saving her sister's life, Celeste seemed lost, taking comfort only
when Odette calmed her into sleep or when she prayed or at-
tended Mass, accompanied each Sunday by a widowed neighbour, Mrs. Bouchard.

When one day Mrs. Bouchard stopped to watch Odette watering some plants on the verandah, she suggested that Celeste might feel "closer to God," as she put it, if she stayed for a few weeks at Our Lady of Mercy Convent, where they had some beds for guests who were having spiritual problems. Mrs. Bouchard said she knew the Mother Superior and, in fact, had gone to school with her. She told Odette she would be happy to talk to the Mother Superior on Celeste's behalf. In the convent Celeste would be closer to others who were devout. She may have been referring to Odette's apostasy, but Odette did not take offence and indeed thought it was an excellent idea. When Celeste heard this, she was delighted and smiled for the first time in weeks. A few days later they went for an interview with the Mother Superior, and Odette was impressed by the order and cleanliness of the rooms, remembering only too well the squalor of that home in St. Henri from which she had rescued her sister twenty years before. Our Lady of Mercy would be an excellent place for Celeste to spend a few weeks to recover her composure. No doubt, the Mother Superior had been informed by Mrs. Bouchard of Odette's apostasy, but she didn't seem particularly critical about it; it was just that in her experience, patients fared better and adjusted to convent life more readily if loved ones visited only twice a week, perhaps Wednesdays and Saturdays.

During that week, James left for Toronto. He had to put his finances in order and he wanted to see Brenda and his grandchildren. He took them to dinner in a restaurant on St. Clair Avenue. Despite the viciousness of that late June evening, his head had now cleared and he felt renewed and enlivened. Ahead of him was a new life with Odette. They had agreed to live together in Quebec City, but they would travel too. They would go to England and Europe, particularly to the Mediterranean, which he had seen and loved as a young man in the 1960s. That evening in the restaurant, he told his family about his future plans with the woman he had fallen in love with when they were teenagers. Brenda was delighted with his new-found happiness, but Gillian, now sixteen, seemed merely bemused with her grandfather's talk about falling in love. Didn't love belong to the young? He sensed that reaction in her wryly amused smile, but he didn't resent it. He would have felt the same at her age. As for Brian at fourteen, he looked merely puzzled by it all.

James promised that he would bring Odette to Toronto for a visit in the near future. He didn't mention the turmoil of the past weeks; to his family it would just seem lurid, something for crime magazines. He knew he was being squeamish about this, but he didn't want them to form an incorrect opinion of Odette. A few days later he returned to Quebec City, and at the end of that week, with Celeste now in Our Lady of Mercy Convent, he and Odette left for Percé. On the train they enjoyed a bottle of wine together and Odette put her hand on his knee and asked, "Do you think we'll be happy together, James?"

He sipped some wine and looked at her. She was recovering at last from Cloutier's attack. Her windpipe had healed and the nightmares had faded. The doctors had said that her heart was fine. She had not really had a heart attack during the assault. He thought she was beginning to look herself again, and he lifted her hand from his knee and kissed it.

"We'll be happy some days and then perhaps on other days we'll have our little moods. I think happiness is largely a matter of temperament, a disposition or attitude, a genetic inheritance.

It helps, of course, if the circumstances in your life are agreeable; if you're not worried about, say, money or health. But some people can still at times feel out of sorts, even when things are going well. At least I do. Why? Because it's the way I am, I suppose. I seem to have a rather melancholic side. My mother was like that, withdrawn and a little sad for no particular reason. It's not clinical depression, it's just a sort of sadness that overtakes you some days. But it passes. You, on the other hand, are much more positive about things, and that's good. I've always admired that about you. The way you overcame that terrible experience in St. Henri when you were only fifteen. And then the loss of your father. Some might have been crushed by that. But you weren't. So we will be fine together, I think. I'll try not to be moody, but no doubt some days I will be."

She put her hand back on his knee.

"On those days, I'll just tell you to go and sulk somewhere else."

"Perfect. But I do believe that our culture is obsessed with happiness and people try too hard to find it. I sometimes think happiness finds you, and you don't need to look for it all the time. For me, on certain days I feel happy. It could come from something as simple as listening to, say, a cardinal singing in a tree on a spring morning. Or maybe from reading a passage from a good book like *The Odyssey*, which I am now reading again. I've reread it nearly every year for I can't remember how long."

"Yes. I've seen you reading this big, thick book. What is this *Odyssey* about?"

"It was written or recited thousands of years ago. It's about a man called Odysseus who leaves the battlefield at Troy and sails for home. He's been away ten years and is tired of war. He misses his wife, Penelope, and his son, Telemachus. This all happened in ancient Greece. He has many adventures on this trip home. After my daughter's death, I would read *The Odyssey* in the middle of the night to keep myself from going mad in search of sleep. I would like to take you to Greece sometime, Odette. I was there in the sixties and I would love to go back."

"I know nothing about this Greek, and you must tell me more about him. And promise you will take me there and to other places and tell me about them."

"Of course. I promise. Cross my heart and hope to die, as we used to say as children."

She laughed. "We used to say that too."

She had leaned into him then, as they listened to the mournful sound of the train whistle announcing itself at a road crossing. "You know, James, I'm really an ignorant woman. I know very little of the world. I've travelled nowhere outside of Quebec. Once, years ago, I went down to New Brunswick. To Moncton, to visit my youngest brother and sister. They are twins and moved away early and married a brother and a sister down there. But that was it. I haven't even been to Ontario. It was mostly Montreal and now Quebec. What a dolt I am."

"You're certainly not a dolt, Odette. You've just had a busy life earning a living, looking after yourself and your sister."

"We'll be sleeping together tonight for the first time," she said, kissing his ear. "Are you going to ravish me tonight, old fella?" She squeezed his arm while she looked out the window. "I'm happy, James. You have made me happy. I miss Celeste, but I am glad she is being looked after by the sisters. It's a very clean place, that convent. And she seems so contented there.

She'll be back home in a few weeks. We must always include my sister in our plans."

"Of course. Celeste will always be a part of our lives."

She had smiled. "I like the way you put that. 'A part of our lives.' "

Then she leaned into him again, putting her head against his shoulder, and he put his arm around her.

"Do you know what I would like you to do tonight?" she asked.

"Nothing too athletic, I hope."

She smiled. "Nothing athletic, no. I will tell you later."

That evening after dinner at the hotel, they went for a walk along the wharf and then returned to the room.

"I want us to take a bath together," she said. "The tub is big. There is room enough for both of us. We must be careful not to slip though. I will get in first and then you can get in behind me."

She gave him a washcloth. "This is nice and soft. Before we get in, I will turn the taps on so that the water is warm but not too hot. No use scolding ourselves."

"Scalding," he said.

"Scalding, of course. A lot of people our age hurt themselves falling in bathtubs, so we must be careful."

In the bathroom they took off their clothes and stood naked before each other.

"Just like Adam and Eve," he said, as he helped her into the tub and then climbed in behind her. The doors were locked against chambermaids turning down beds and leaving chocolates by the pillows. Her voice was still a little husky where Cloutier's hands had damaged her throat and windpipe.

"Wash my back very gently. There is still a little bruising there. When you have finished, I want you to reach around and wash my breasts and stomach. Very gently, please. Then wash below that. I want you to put your fingers inside me, and please do so again gently. I will lean back against you while you are doing this. Now nice and easy. Okay?"

"Yes, of course. And I will kiss your back too. And the back of your neck and ears."

"That will be nice. Yes. Lots of kissing. We must use our tongues on each other." He gently massaged her pubis and then inside and she moaned softly with pleasure. "Yes, yes, that's good."

After she took his hand away, she got up and carefully got out of the tub. There above him was the body he had dreamt of touching so many times that summer. Now aged and the breasts pendulous, but still wonderfully alluring. Her body had been much used by other men over the years, but it was still desirable. Then in the white hotel kimono she knelt by the side of the tub and took the washcloth and washed his penis, smiling. When he got carefully to his feet and out of the tub, she dried him off slowly, put the hotel bathrobe on him, and took his hand into bed. There she took the robes off both of them, and when he was on his back, she leaned down and slowly, carefully, enticingly put her hand between his thighs while she fellated him. They were making love at their ages! How wonderful! he thought.

What, he wondered, must she have been like at nineteen or twenty? And so much of it wasted on that brute Cloutier. She had opened her eyes and smiled at him then. "I could have a heart attack doing this at my age."

"It occurred to me that I could too."

"Imagine if we both went out doing this and they found us the next morning. What a story for the newspapers, eh?"

"I've waited a long time for tonight."

She passed a finger over his lips. "You must read some of that Greek book to me some night. But not tonight. I'm ready to sleep now and so should you be."

"How does it feel to be back in this hotel some sixty years later?"

"It feels a little strange, and they've changed the whole interior. It's actually much nicer. I remember smaller rooms. I think they were smaller, anyway. It's funny. When I left the village that summer, I never imagined that I would see this place again, let alone sleep here. This afternoon when we arrived, I saw a young woman changing the sheets in a room. Did you see her, James?"

"I don't think so."

"Well, you were looking for the number of our room, I guess, and the door to this room was only half open. But I couldn't help noticing this young woman doing what I used to do. I felt like telling her that I once did that, but I didn't. It was so long ago and it's over. Let's go to sleep."

But in the night she awakened. The clock on the bedside table said three-thirty. For a moment she didn't know where she was. James was on his side, facing away from her. She was going to reach out but didn't want to awaken him. The sex had been . . . what was the word? When you drink tea that has been in the cup too long. It's not hot enough. What was that word? *Tepid.* That was the word. To please him, she had moaned a little, but it was not the same. How could it be at their age? And James seemed a

little shy about it. Was that the word? *Shy*? Yes. She guessed that
he hadn't known many women. But he was kind and it was good
to have the comfort of someone to love and to share whatever
time was left to them. She felt herself quite suddenly saddened
and tearful. So much now was over. Finished. She thought of
Marcel Dubé, an old love who had taken her to that hotel on
Sherbrooke Street, where he had run a bath for them. They had
drunk some wine and then washed each other and made such
love that night. She could still remember the noise of the rain
filling the eavestroughs by the open window. Poor Marcel, who
had died in his fifties from cancer all those years ago. In many
ways, she thought, Celeste was better off; her sister lived to die
and see God and Heaven, while she herself could only imagine
the end of everything. And how much time was left before that?
A few more years, if she was lucky. She felt such a surge of un-
ease that she rolled over and put her arms around James. Rested
her cheek against his back. He stirred faintly but didn't awaken.
In a few hours they would get ready for the day. They were
going to the village where she had spent the summer with her
family. My God, she thought, I was only fifteen. Was it really a
good idea to return to such places from your younger days? Perhaps it depended on circumstances. That young woman she had
seen cleaning a room—what was ahead of her? They still hired
women to clean rooms. There was no machine for making beds,
and you never saw a man doing it. But such jobs led nowhere.
Yet perhaps she was a student and this was only summer work,
though she had looked older. Maybe her husband has lost his
job and she is helping the family. Odette didn't think the young
woman was just a girl from St. Henri who was cleaning rooms
that summer and knew she was pregnant, ahead of her a dismal

room and a woman with the rubber hosing for her to bite on and a girl reading a comic book and eating Cracker Jacks.

She could feel James's ribs. A lean, elderly man. Still handsome, with that air of sadness he had talked about. But then he had lost his wife and daughter. What a terrible blow late in life. To outlive a child. She had been callous in not asking him more about his family, though she sensed that he kept these griefs to himself. Still, it would have been at the very least polite to inquire. When she put her arm around him, he stirred again but only briefly. It felt good to share the bed with him.

• •

He awakened to the ringing of the bedside telephone. It was on Odette's side, and when he turned, she was already sitting up with her back to him, listening to the message. He looked at his watch. Ten minutes to six. A phone call at this hour was surely bad news. And who even knew they were staying at this hotel? He tried to remember whom Odette had told of their plans. Odette was speaking French to the caller, and he caught only the word "merci" as she hung up the receiver. When she turned to him, however, she was weeping with both hands to her face, the tears leaking through her fingers, and he thought he knew why. "What is it, Odette? Is it Celeste?" She nodded a yes and reached for tissues on the bedside table. He moved over and embraced her. "Tell me what's happened."

"That was the Mother Superior at the convent," she said. "When one of the sisters looked in on Celeste this morning, she thought she was still sleeping, but something didn't look right, and when she went over to her, she could see that she was gone." Odette began to weep. "We so wanted to say goodbye to one another. We talked about it many times. She always asked me if I would be there by her side holding her hand when the time came. And now she's gone and I wasn't there holding her hand." She leaned back again weeping, holding more tissue to her eyes. "We have to go back today. I should never have come here. It was a mistake to leave her like that. I should have stayed closer to her." She was trembling as he held her.

"You couldn't have done anything about it even if you had been in your own house. I'm very sorry, believe me, but there is nothing you could have done. She simply died in her sleep. She didn't suffer at the end. That has to be a comfort to you. Was it her heart?"

"Yes, that's what they think. That goddamn Raoul trying to choke me to death on the kitchen floor, and she must have strained her heart when she tried to help me. How could she not, for God's sake? She was a frail eighty-one-year-old woman. She was never the same after that. It took a lot out of her. It must have."

"Yes. I'm sure it did."

"We have to go back now."

"Of course we do," he said, getting out of bed. "Please just stay where you are for a while. I'm going to have a quick shower and dress and go down to the front desk and ask about flying back to Quebec City. They have an airport near Gaspé town. I'll see when the next flight leaves. It's still early, and with any luck, we'll get a flight out today and be there in two or three hours."

"I don't know where to begin," she said, wiping her eyes. "There is so much to do. I have to get in touch with our sisters. And find a funeral director."

He sat down beside her and took her hand. "Look, we'll deal with all that. But one day at a time, Odette. That is how I tried to get through my wife's death and my daughter's. We'll work this out, but first we must get back to Quebec City." He kissed the top of her head. "All right?"

She nodded a yes. "I'm so glad you are here with me."

"Well, I'm glad to be with you too. I'll go downstairs and see what I can find out about flying to Quebec City today. I'll rent a car to get us there, and if there is no rental agency in Percé, we'll take a taxi to the airport."

She offered only a thin smile, but at least it was a smile. "Okay, James."

"While I'm down there, I'll arrange for breakfast to be brought up. What do you want?"

"I don't care. I'm not hungry."

"That's not helpful. You have to eat something. It's going to be a busy day."

All she could do was nod her head and wipe her eyes. He kissed her again.

"I'll get something for both of us. We'll do all of this together today. Okay?"

He had another thin smile from her as he kissed her damp face.

• •

The church was a cool refuge from the late morning sun. He was seated halfway down the main aisle, next to Odette's niece, Danielle McCann. He had met her outside the church, a tall blond woman in her late forties or possibly older, for when she took off her sunglasses, he noticed the little crow's feet at the corner of her eyes. But she was still a handsome woman with a smile that put him in mind of Odette. Offering her hand, she said, "You must be Professor Hillyer."

"I'm very glad to meet you and I must thank you again for your help, but please call me James. My days as a professor are well behind me now."

For a moment they watched others entering the church. "My aunt told me you two are planning a trip to Europe."

"Indeed we are," he said, "in late August or early September, when the heat and the summer tourists are gone."

"How wonderful. It sounds like a honeymoon." There was that coquettish smile again.

"We're looking forward to it. We're going first to Toronto to spend a few days with my son's family. And then we'll fly to New York and take a ship to Italy and Greece."

"Well, good for you both. I wish you well." She looked again at the open church door. "May I sit with you? I'm a bit of an outsider myself. With the family, I mean. Like Aunty Odette."

"By all means," he said.

As they were being seated, he looked ahead just as Odette turned, perhaps to find him, and then she smiled. As he watched and listened to the ceremony, he thought of how isolated Odette was from her family. She sat in the front row in the aisle seat at least three or four spaces from the nearest family member.

The night before, as they had lain in bed at home, Odette had been fretting, telling him about her sisters and nieces and how they had treated her over the years: how they had spread rumours about her, complained about her extravagance and deplorable taste in men. She told him she had made it clear that

they would not be welcome in her house when they arrived for
Celeste's funeral. They would have to find a hotel or return to
Montreal the same day. "I don't give a damn," she said. "I don't
want them in my house."

He had been tired and on the verge of sleep, listening to
her all the same. He supposed she needed to get it off her chest.
"When I moved into this house last winter, James, I invited
them all down. I wasn't trying to show off, but I knew they
wanted to see where I lived now. They had told me so. But
all they did was talk about how much everything must have
cost. I remember I was in the kitchen making dinner and they
were going through the house, and all they could talk about
was how much everything must have cost. All I could hear was
the word 'extravagant' over and over again. 'Oh, that must have
cost a fortune.' Or 'Why would Odette need that?' Well, the
money was mine and Celeste's, goddamn it, and we were going
to enjoy it after all those years in cold-water flats in St. Henri.
Not once in those years did anyone invite us for Christmas
dinner. Sylvie and Lucille have held a grudge against me all
their lives, and they've passed it on to their kids. Why shouldn't
I have a little luxury now after all these years, goddamn it to
hell?"

He had put his arm around her. "You're getting yourself
worked up. Try to calm down a bit. Have a little of this brandy.
It will help you to sleep."

Sitting up, she had drunk some brandy and then lain back,
holding the glass on her chest.

"I dread tomorrow," she had said. "Sitting with all of them
at the front of the church." After drinking a little more brandy,
she had added, "I'll bet right now they are talking about me,

telling one another that I shouldn't have gone to Gaspé with you and left Celeste by herself in the city."

"Nonsense," he had said, "they knew she was well looked after in that convent. She died peacefully in her sleep. It was nobody's fault, least of all yours. You must calm down and try to get some sleep. Tomorrow will be an important day for you. You will be there for Celeste. Never mind your sisters and nieces."

She had finished her brandy and handed him the glass. But he might as well have been talking to the wallpaper. "After the service tomorrow," she had said, "there will be a luncheon served by the Women's Guild or whatever they're called. I certainly wasn't going to make sandwiches for them. I'll be damned if I was." He must have sighed then, for she had looked over at him and taken his hand. "Yes, yes, you are right, old fellow. We have to get some sleep, don't we? Give me a kiss and I'll shut up."

Now in the church he looked at the back of her head and at the backs of her relatives farther along the pew, thinking of the spite that smoulders on through some families for years, old grudges that are probably taken to the grave. All that time wasted on malice. It left him feeling grateful that he had been an only child. He was thinking too of Celeste in the dark brown coffin by the altar, her life one long imprisonment in childhood, and of Odette's love and devotion to her sister's plight. Now Celeste was in the dark silence, as shall we all be one day, he thought. But before then, however, he and Odette would have some time together. And it must be time well spent.

Envoi

Odette and James had seven good years together before he died from congestive heart failure in the late autumn of 2013. He was eighty-three. As I write this, my aunt Odette is still with us in a retirement home in Quebec City, deaf in one ear, but otherwise in good health for her age. She will be eighty-five in December. When I visited her recently, she told me that she was happy enough. "It does no good," she said, "to dwell too long on the loss of a loved one, for loss is a part of life." But each year, on the anniversary of James's death, she intends to read again Homer's *Odyssey*, remembering her journeys with James to London and Paris, to Venice and Rome and other cities, but especially their visit to Athens and the Greek islands, ever grateful for those last seven years together.

ACKNOWLEDGMENTS

I would like to thank my editor, Phyllis Bruce, and my agent, Dean Cooke, for their support and encouragement over the years.